Books by Jean Thesman

The Moonstones

by Jean Thesman

VIKING

S.
T 343ms

VIKING
Published by the Penguin Group
Penguin Putnam Books for Young Readers, 345 Hudson Street, New York,
New York 10014, U.S.A.
Penguin Books Ltd, 27 Wrights Lane, London W8 5TZ, England
Penguin Books Australia Ltd, Ringwood, Victoria, Australia
Penguin Books Canada Ltd, 10 Alcorn Avenue, Toronto, Ontario, Canada M4V 3B2
Penguin Books (N.Z.) Ltd, 182–190 Wairau Road, Auckland 10, New Zealand

Penguin Books Ltd, Registered Offices: Harmondsworth, Middlesex, England

First published in 1998 by Viking, a member of Penguin Putnam Books
for Young Readers.

1   3   5   7   9   10   8   6   4   2

LIBRARY OF CONGRESS CATALOGING-IN-PUBLICATION DATA:
Thesman, Jean.
The moonstones / Jean Thesman.
p.   cm.
Summary: While helping her mother clean out the family home in Puget Sound, fifteen-
year-old Jane must deal with her hateful aunt and difficult cousin Ricki, a romance that
cannot last, and secrets from her mother's past.
ISBN 0-670-87959-2 (hardcover)
1. Cousins—Fiction.   2. Aunts—Fiction.   3. Mothers and daughters—Fiction.
4. Puget Sound (Wash.)—Fiction.]   I. Title.
PZ7.T3525Mr   1998   [Fic]—dc21   97-52307   CIP   AC

Printed in the U.S.A.
Set in Garamond

But you were something more than young and sweet
And fair,—and the long year remembers you.

EDNA ST. VINCENT MILLAY, *COLLECTED SONNETS*

To the little girl with red hair

BROWN-HEADED COWBIRD *MOLOTHRUS ATER*

This member of the blackbird family is a brood
parasite. The female lays an egg in the nest of a
smaller bird. When the large cowbird chick
hatches, it forces the smaller chicks out of the
nest, where they starve and die.

Chapter One

I watched them descending the path to the beach, barely visible in the blue and shadowless twilight. I had seen the three boys and two girls the evening before as they hurried past the tall iron fence that separated Grandmother's house from the woods and Puget Sound. This small old town, Royal Bay, seemed to be at the end of the world, and so far nothing in it interested me—except one boy.

"Hello again," I whispered. "Hello, you with the gray eyes."

He followed a few steps behind the other four, but he didn't seem to be a *follower*. There was something about the set of his square shoulders and his erect posture that made me think he did as he pleased. I liked that. He didn't swagger, but I was certain that he had all the self-confidence I wished I had. I hoped that he would look back at the house, but even more, I hoped that he remembered seeing me in town the day Mom and I arrived.

But what would be the point? Even if we became acquainted, I wouldn't be there long enough for us to be friends. The truth was that I couldn't wait to get back to Seattle.

From my bedroom window, I watched the amusement park lights

far down the beach, strings of bright glitter that made the ugly place look like fairyland at night. I was certain that the five kids were going there. I didn't know what attracted them to it, because by daylight, it looked tacky and a little dangerous. Mom had already warned me against going there, not that she needed to worry about it.

Were the kids tourists in Royal Bay? Mom had said that the tourist season really didn't begin until the last week of June. The sun might come out between rain showers, but that didn't mean warm weather, not on this part of Puget Sound.

Maybe they lived in the dreary town all year, I thought, feeling sorry for them. They were almost out of sight then, near the bottom of the steep path at the edge of the woods.

The boy with dark hair and gray eyes had not looked back. I was disappointed. And I was tired, too, because I had worked hard all day. I wanted to go home.

"Jane?"

I glanced over my shoulder. Mom stood in the doorway, the light from the hall silhouetting her narrow body. "Honey, why are you standing there in the dark?" she asked.

I reached out to turn on the small desk lamp next to me. "I was spying on some kids going down to the beach," I said. "Who do you suppose they could be?"

"They're from town, probably," she said. "Tourists usually don't find the path. I came up to see if you're hungry."

"Starved," I said. "Maybe we should eat. It doesn't look like Aunt Norma and Rhonda are coming today, either."

"Probably I should have had the phone put back in," Mom said.

"Then Norma could have let me know what's keeping her. Okay, Jane, let's leave. Do you want to go back to the spaghetti restaurant?"

"No, let's try a different place," I said as I grabbed my denim jacket. "Let's go out on the town tonight."

Mom appreciated the joke.

My mother, Abby Douglas, and I had come from Seattle to Royal Bay to get the house ready for sale. Grandmother had died two years before, and except for Mr. and Mrs. Phare, the neighbors who had volunteered to watch over the place, no one had been inside since then. The estate was taking a long time to settle.

I had not wanted to go to Royal Bay with Mom. I had made plans with my best friend, Kitty Vernon, for the first days of summer vacation. We had signed up for swim classes and wanted to volunteer at the zoo. I had watched Mom pack, and she didn't give even a hint that she needed company on the trip. But during dinner the night before she planned to leave, she suddenly asked me to go with her.

"Please," she said, and her expression surprised me. My efficient mother, the college math teacher, never seemed insecure or uncertain. Her unfamiliar, worried frown made me feel uneasy.

"Please come," she said. "I'll show you around the place where I grew up. We'll have fun."

I doubted that, but I agreed to go, especially after I saw Dad's encouraging nod.

I had been right. Royal Bay wasn't much fun. And Mom almost seemed to be as much a stranger in the old cannery town as I was.

I'd expected her to be greeting people on every street corner, but when I asked her if she planned to look up old friends, she explained that people moved away as soon as they finished high school. She hadn't kept track of anybody.

We decided to walk the half mile to town. As we passed the Phare house next door, they pulled into their driveway and called out to us.

"Norma still hasn't shown up?" Mrs. Phare asked. She had known both Mom and Aunt Norma since they were girls.

"Not yet," Mom called back.

"Isn't that just like her?" Mrs. Phare said, her voice sharp. "Abby, why don't you hire somebody to clean the house, and send Norma the bill." She didn't wait for a response, but went in her side door.

"As if Norma would pay it," Mom muttered to herself.

Grandmother hadn't left a will, but Dad said that it wouldn't have helped, because Aunt Norma was in the crisis business.

"If one doesn't already exist, she'll find a way to fill the gap," Dad had said.

Once, to put an end to the arguing, Mom had offered to give Norma everything, but my aunt complained that Mom was trying to make her look bad. I couldn't imagine who would care. Finally, after two long years, a court told them what to do—sell everything except for a few keepsakes and divide the money.

Aunt Norma changed her mind a dozen times about when she

could come to Royal Bay to go through the house. Finally she settled on a date, but she still hadn't shown up.

I barely remembered her and her daughter, Rhonda, who was my age, fifteen. I hadn't seen them for nine years. I had always been close to Dad's large family in Seattle, so I rarely gave a thought to my two relatives in California. If they didn't show up, I wouldn't care.

We walked briskly toward the restaurant. On the cliff behind the town, big new houses with glass walls stared down over the marina, the cheap new motels with their bright blue pools, the dozens of small shops that opened only during the summer months, and the six—I counted them—antique stores.

I had first seen the tall, gray-eyed boy standing outside Boone's Antique Shop. Now, as we passed it on the way to the restaurant, I remembered how he had stared at me that day with something like shock on his face, as if he had seen me before but had never expected to see me again.

I had stared, too, into those luminous eyes shadowed by long black lashes. The boy was as dark as I was fair, his smooth skin already tanned, his hair a little too long, while I was pale blond like my mother, with straight hair and blue eyes. I had thought he was—gorgeous. When he smiled, I could scarcely breathe.

What was he doing in that awful town? He was like someone out of a daydream. I hadn't had many boyfriends and none of them had made such an impact on first sight.

Remembering, I blushed as I hurried with Mom toward the restaurant, and I hoped she didn't notice.

"You're awfully quiet," Mom said. "Are you sorry you came with me? I could have asked your dad, too, but if he took vacation time for this, we couldn't go to Canada in August."

"I'll survive the town," I said. "But I wish Aunt Norma would show up and do her share of the work."

The restaurant was half full, and the waitress seated us right away. Across the room from us, a large family was celebrating someone's birthday. Mom watched with an unreadable expression. Once she had said that when she was a child, she and her mother and sister had never celebrated anything. Mom's father had died when she was small, and Grandmother grieved for the rest of her life. That was almost all I knew about my mother's childhood.

Earlier that year, on a rainy afternoon at Kitty's house, her mother had let us look through a thick scrapbook she had kept during high school. We spent an hour going over it, examining the dance cards and movie ticket stubs, the concert programs, the notes, and crumbling pressed flowers. There were snapshots of Mrs. Vernon when she was fourteen and getting ready to go out on her first date, and dressed for her first prom at fifteen. We smiled over pictures of her with a dozen different boys, taken when she was skiing or ice-skating, swimming, and playing tennis. On the last page we found her graduation program and a picture of her in a long dress with a blond boy smiling at her.

That night I asked Mom if she had kept a scrapbook, but she said she hadn't. It didn't surprise me. She was different from Mrs. Vernon, who was sentimental and emotional.

In the restaurant, a brown-haired boy in a white shirt and a red vest cleared cups and dessert plates from the table next to us. He saw me and grinned.

"Don't order stuffed pork chops," he said in a conspiratorial tone. "My uncle is the chef, but he's crabby tonight, so who knows what he's stuffed them with? Try salmon instead."

"Owen!" a woman shouted from behind the counter.

"Duck," the boy said to me. "That's my mother, and she's out on bail this week. A big mistake." He picked up the tray of dishes and hurried away, laughing.

"Owen, I'm not telling you one more time . . ." the woman behind the counter said. Her voice trailed away as she followed the boy through a doorway.

"Well, *he's* cute," Mom said, looking at me over the top of her menu. "Don't you think so?"

He was, but he reminded me of the boys in my school and the boys I'd dated. Not very grown-up. Not the least bit exciting.

And I couldn't get the other boy's gray eyes off my mind. The eyes and the stare and the slow, delicious smile of surprise, as if he had recognized me.

Owen was back. "Mom and the waitress had a small disagreement and someone's taking them both to the hospital, so I'll be your waiter tonight." He handed me a daisy exactly like the ones in the small bouquet on our table. I put the daisy in a buttonhole in my jacket.

The woman bore down on him and snatched the back of his collar. "I'm very sorry," she told Mom and me. "We're new here and my son's life's work is ruining our reputations in one place after another." She hissed something at him, but he winked at me until she yanked his ear.

"Ow, ow, ow!" he yelled as he hurried away. "Child abuse!" The people sitting closest to us laughed aloud.

Owen's mother was red-faced. "I apologize again," she said. "I'd kill him, but I don't want to stay in this town long enough to be put on trial for it. We're helping out here until my sister-in-law gets out of the hospital, and then we'll go back to Seattle, I promise."

Mom laughed. "Maybe we'll see you there, then," she said. "We're here only for a week."

"Owen will probably ruin it for you," the woman said. "Did he mention the salmon? It's really wonderful, but my brother fixes marvelous stuffed pork chops."

I suppressed a smile.

Owen was back, carrying two glasses of water and slopping much of it on the carpet. He shook his head violently when his mother said "pork chops."

"Want to go to a movie?" he said as he put down my glass. "There's a theater in Port Shasta. Or we could get married and I could come and live with you. At least *your* mother doesn't look like she'd have a lot of tattoos."

I couldn't help but laugh, which clearly delighted him but disgusted his mother. "You're fired," she told him. "Go back to the house right this instant."

"Don't you wish," the boy said to her. "What's your name?" he asked me.

I told him, grinning.

"I'm Owen Norris," he said. "And I'm available for anything."

"But I'm not," I shot right back. "Mind your mother."

"I love sassy girls," he said as he walked away.

We were the last customers, and the restaurant was nearly empty by the time we finished our dinners. Owen and his mother brought dessert to the table and sat down with us.

I learned that he went to a high school on the north side of Seattle, was a year ahead of me, and played soccer. He said he'd call me when he got home, but that probably wouldn't be until after the Fourth of July.

"You won't move to New Zealand before that, will you?" he asked. "I'd like to see you again."

"I'm leaving for music camp on the tenth of July," I said as I watched him scrape the last of the frosting off his plate. "But it's not in New Zealand."

"I can wait until you get back," he said. He pushed his plate away. "Believe me, I can wait. In the meantime, do you want to do something tomorrow?"

I smiled, but I shook my head. "I'm helping Mom get my grandmother's house ready to sell, and we've got a lot of work to do in a week. But thanks for asking."

"You can take a few hours . . ." Mom began.

I gave her a sideways look and she stopped. "We'll see," I said.

Owen dropped the subject and concentrated on teasing his mother, to my relief. But I enjoyed listening to him.

Suddenly we were startled by a voice as sharp as a slap. "Abby, where have you been!" Aunt Norma cried.

I had forgotten about Aunt Norma and Rhonda. Their abrupt appearance shocked me into silence.

Mom flushed when she looked up. "Norma! When did you get here?"

"We're locked out of the house!" Aunt Norma rattled on as if she hadn't heard. "We sat there in the dark, starving, and finally decided we'd give up on you and find a meal and a place to stay. But I counted on you, Abby, and *now* look what you've done."

Mrs. Norris and Owen got up and slipped away tactfully. I knew I was blushing as hard as Mom. Both of us hate people who make scenes in public.

My cousin Rhonda stood behind her mother. Her small brown eyes shifted constantly, from Mom to me to Owen, who had busied himself behind the counter. Her dark hair was stiffly styled, and her lashes were thick with mascara. Her red skirt was so short that I wondered what would happen if she dropped her purse and there was no one around to pick it up.

"Hello, Rhonda," I said firmly, trying to drown out Aunt Norma's whining.

"I'm called Ricki now," my cousin said, her voice high as a

child's. She smiled, showing perfect small teeth. "That boy you were sitting with—he's pretty cute. When did you meet him?"

For some reason, I didn't want to tell her anything about Owen. But that would have been rude. "That's Owen," I said. "He and his mother are here helping out for a while."

Rhonda—Ricki—made a small, satisfied sound.

"Norma, I'm starved," she told her mother. "Let's order something before the place closes."

Aunt Norma had been fussing with her yellow hair. Sighing, she snapped her gold compact closed. "Can we have some service here?" she called out imperiously. She snapped her fingers and her diamond rings, two on each hand, glittered. "Service, somebody!"

The pale family prettiness of my mother and even my grandmother had turned to brass with Norma. But she wore beautiful clothes, and her handbag probably cost more than my clothes allowance for a whole year. My California relatives looked rich. They certainly were glamorous.

Mrs. Norris hurried to the table with menus. Owen had disappeared.

"So, *Janie*," Ricki said, leaning forward and resting her elbows on the table. She smiled, showing her sharp little teeth. "What have you been doing for fun around here?"

Chapter Two

After Aunt Norma and Ricki ate, we drove back to the house in their rental car. Ricki and I sat in silence, looking out our windows at the dark streets. I couldn't remember ever feeling more uncomfortable.

While she drove, Aunt Norma complained about the rental car, the flight from Los Angeles to Seattle, and the burden of spending time in an old dusty house when she could have gone on a "fabulous" cruise with her "fabulous" friends. Ricki nudged me and rolled her eyes.

Once in the house, Aunt Norma looked around and sighed. "This place hasn't changed a bit. But at least you've done a little cleaning."

A *little* cleaning? Why didn't Mom say anything? We had worked hard on the downstairs rooms, and they shone with wax and polish.

But Mom didn't respond.

As if noticing Ricki for the first time since they walked into the house, Aunt Norma said, "Do something to make yourself useful, Ricki. Go out to the car and get our bags out of the trunk."

Ricki caught the keys her mother tossed and started for the door. I followed, saying, "I'll help."

They had brought four big suitcases and two carry-on bags, but two of the suitcases seemed so light that I suspected they were empty. They must have planned to take home lots of keepsakes.

Back inside, we heard Aunt Norma from the other end of the hall. "Do you mean she actually wasted money on a new kitchen before she died?"

"The realtor said it will make the house easier to sell," Mom said soothingly.

"Oh, sure, they *always* say things like that. Why do you trust strangers?"

Ricki dropped the bags she'd carried in and yelled, "Norma, I'm tired. Where's my bedroom?"

Her mother ignored her, but my mother hurried through the dining room. "You're sharing with Jane," she said. "Only two of the bedrooms are furnished."

"Suits me," Ricki said. "I hate sharing a room with Norma, because she snores."

My cousin grabbed a suitcase and one of the carry-on bags and started for the stairs. When I didn't follow, she looked back and said, "Which room?"

"Oh," I blurted. "Sorry. I'll show you. We've got the room in back, overlooking the beach. You'll like it, but I'm afraid it's still a little dusty. We haven't—"

"Whatever," Ricki interrupted. "I'm so tired I don't care where I sleep."

"Goodnight, Ricki," Mom said. "Jane, are you turning in now, too?"

It was late, and suddenly I was exhausted. "I might as well," I said as I started up. "Goodnight, everybody."

I heard Aunt Norma come into the hall. She didn't bother saying goodnight to Ricki and me, but instead began questioning Mom about the china in the dining room buffet. "Is that all that's left of her Royal Doulton china?" she asked. "Did you take some of it?"

"Of course not," Mom said firmly. "If it's here, we'll find it."

"If the Phares didn't steal it," Aunt Norma said.

I hurried to get away. On the second floor, I led Ricki to our room, expecting her to take the unused twin bed by the wall. But she snatched my pajamas off the bed by the window, tossed them to the other bed, and said, "I have to sleep by a window. I'm claustrophobic."

"Oh," I said.

She dropped her suitcase and tossed her other bag on the bed. "I hate having curtains closed," she said, and she yanked them back.

A little dust fell out of the folds, but she didn't comment on it. She sat on the edge of her bed and examined her dark red fingernails.

"I've chipped my nail polish," she said disgustedly. "I had these done the day before yesterday, and they're ruined already."

She glanced at my hands and pretended to shudder. "Can't you grow your nails?" she asked.

"I play the violin," I said, already knowing what she'd say next. I'd heard it before.

"Bor-ing," she drawled. She jumped up and pushed open the window. "What's that? An amusement park? Have you been there? I love amusement parks. Let's check it out."

I looked over her shoulder and saw the lights, some whirling around, some draped in ropes and strands. The park seemed to be alive—and thrilling. But the Sound seemed as black as the edge of the universe and every bit as ominous. The contrast made the amusement park even more inviting. The lights were pushing back an unknowable dark, and there was music there, and even other kids. . . . And the gray-eyed boy.

"I suppose we could ask if it's okay," I said doubtfully.

"You're kidding, right?" Ricki said. "Norma is barely speaking to me this week. But that doesn't mean we can't go. We'll just sneak out after they go to bed. Where's their room?"

I almost hated telling her. It made everything too easy. "Their room is at the other end of the hall, around the corner by the bathroom."

"Away from the stairs?" Ricki asked.

I nodded.

Ricki hugged herself. "Great," she said. "Norma is going deaf, although she won't admit it. We can get out without any problems."

"*My* mother isn't deaf," I said. But Mom was tired. She'd fall asleep the instant she crawled into bed.

Part of me was excited, but part of me was wary. I'd never sneaked out on my parents. I'd never even considered it. And I'd never been to a place like an amusement park with only another girl, after dark, in a strange town.

15

But probably *he* was there, that gray-eyed boy. Maybe I'd see him again. Maybe he'd even come up and talk to me. Anything was possible, I thought, if I had the courage to step out and take a chance.

Ricki unzipped her suitcase and took out a small radio, which she turned on at full volume. Then she pulled out clothes, tossing everything on the floor. She held up a skimpy white sundress. "Do you like this?"

"You'll freeze," I said. "It's cold tonight."

"I can put this over it," she said, holding up a fuzzy red sweater.

"I'll wear what I've got on," I said.

She eyed my jeans and denim jacket. "Suit yourself," she said, shrugging.

She had a lot to learn about the climate.

"Maybe you'd better turn off the radio," I said. "They might come in to complain about the noise."

"You worry about everything, don't you?" she asked.

"One of us has to," I said, laughing a little.

She laughed, too, but she turned off her radio.

My cousin was adventurous and flamboyant, but she might be the key to the boy I liked too much before ever having met him.

Ordinarily, I wouldn't have thought that half an hour was very long, but that night it was. We could hear our mothers talking downstairs, but we weren't interested. I stood at the window, watching the amusement park lights, while Ricki fussed with her hair.

Aunt Norma didn't bother with us. I heard her come up and

slam the bathroom door. Mom came up two minutes later, rapped on our door, and said, "Goodnight, girls."

We answered cheerfully, grinning at each other.

Ricki, preening in front of the mirror on the closet door, asked, "Do you have a boyfriend?"

"Shh," I said.

"Right," she whispered as she pulled the red sweater down snugly over her hips. "But do you?"

"Have a boyfriend? No, not right now. Do you?"

"Of course," Ricki said. "But that doesn't mean I can't have fun while I'm here. I don't think I could stand it, not even for a couple of days, if I couldn't find something to do. I like to keep on the move, you know?"

I nodded, but I was still thinking about something she'd said. "A couple of days."

"How long are you staying here?" I asked slowly.

She was applying mascara now, over the mascara she already wore. "Like I said," she said. "A couple of days. We're not big on cleaning houses. And Norma hates this town. She just wants to get some stuff, and then we're out of here."

I wanted to say, "She's supposed to help." But I didn't.

There was something about my cousin, something not very nice, but intriguing. She was silly and shallow, but I had a hunch she *knew* things, and I didn't want to alienate her.

She crossed to the windows, looked out, and sighed. "We're missing all the fun. Can we climb down some way? Is there a lattice, something like that?"

I stared. "No, I don't think so. We'll have to use the stairs."

"Oh, pooh," she said, pouting. The expression was wasted on me, but I knew that a boy would make himself crazy trying to please her, and never resent her for a moment.

We heard the bathroom door open and close twice, and then Mom's bedroom door shut and the house was silent.

"Let's go," Ricki said.

"They couldn't be asleep this fast," I said.

"But they're probably busy arguing in whispers so they won't wake us," she said. "They won't hear anything else."

I thought she was terribly wise.

Before we left the room, she said, "Take off your shoes and stay on the side of the steps, as close to the wall as you can. That way they won't squeak."

She was right. We crept down barefoot, and no one could have heard anything except, perhaps, the hammering of my heart. Outside, I showed her where the path was, running beside Grandmother's tall fence.

There was a lopsided moon in the sky, but it didn't give us enough light, so we stumbled along the unfamiliar path, stifling our laughter until we were sure we were far enough away that our mothers couldn't hear us.

My best friend, Kitty, was the exact opposite of my cousin. She was bright and responsible, with a dry sort of humor. There was no way in this world that she would have agreed to sneak out on our mothers so we could run down a rocky beach in the dark to a cheap amusement park. Kitty was a big believer in avoiding punishment. So was I.

But Ricki's daring giggle was contagious. And I couldn't forget the tall boy with gray eyes.

Now I was sorry that I was wearing nothing better than old jeans and a denim jacket.

As we drew closer to the amusement park, we crossed into the circle of brightness cast by the lights. Ricki asked me how she looked as she stopped to fuss with her hair again.

Didn't she know? "You look great," I said. "I'm the one who looks awful."

"You're right," she said. I could tell that she actually meant it. It didn't bother her to say something that rude. "You could have changed clothes, but I don't mind that you didn't. I don't like competition. In fact, I don't like girls very much."

She darted up the stone steps set into the sea wall, and without waiting for me, got in line at the entrance of the amusement park. I followed, hurt, angry with her, with myself, and with whatever alien impulse cancelled out my common sense and sent me sneaking out of the house with this birdbrain in her too-tight clothes. And I was a little jealous.

There wasn't as big a crowd inside as I had expected, but it was late on a weeknight, and the tourist season hadn't started yet. I saw a lot of teenagers there, though. Royal Bay couldn't have had so many. It wouldn't have surprised me if I met other kids from Seattle.

I tried to walk beside Ricki, but she kept a little ahead of me, swinging her hips, occasionally tossing back a word to me the way someone tosses treats to a dog. Was this deliberate? No, probably not. She was self-centered because she was good-looking and glamorous. And she hardly knew me.

"Let's ride the Ferris wheel," she said. "Then we can look over everything."

We started toward the ticket booth, but before we got there, she stopped to watch two boys playing a video game near the entrance of an arcade. I was sure they were the boys who had walked down the path earlier with the two girls and the gray-eyed boy. My heart seemed to beat in my throat.

"Hey, there," one of the boys said to Ricki. "Where are you going?"

"Wherever the fun is," Ricki said. She didn't look directly at him, but instead glanced around as if she was waiting for someone exciting.

The boy fell for it. "You meeting a guy here?" he asked. He wasn't much taller than she was, but he had a cocky way about him, a way of grinning that was too knowing, and he ran his fingers through his sandy hair too often. He wore a leather jacket, and he was cute. He was also a little scary.

Ricki laughed. "Do I look like a girl who would wait for anybody?"

The boy visibly relaxed. He knew that game. "Is your name as cute as you are?" he asked.

"You bet," Ricki said. "I'm Ricki Goodwin. How about you?"

He was Dennis Sherman, he said, and his friend was Pete Striker. Ricki told them my name, but neither of them paid any attention. Pete, tall and blond, fixed his attention on the game he played. A cigarette dangled from his lower lip. He seemed angry.

"You guys here with anybody?" Ricki asked. I was sure she was asking about girls; she didn't like competition. I wasn't likely to forget that.

"Pete's sister is here," Dennis said. "She's Ellie. And Meg Floyd is around somewhere."

"They went to the cafe with Carey," Pete growled. "Remember? You sent them there for something to drink."

Dennis grinned at Ricki again. "Meeting you wiped out everything in my mind," he said.

"I should hope so," Ricki said.

The boys didn't notice me. I wished I'd stayed home. I wished my mother had caught me sneaking down the stairs and grounded me for the rest of my life. I wished I was dead.

Then there he was, the gray-eyed boy, walking toward me, carrying a paper cup. He wore a black jacket and a white shirt that showed off his tan.

"It's you," he said, and he blinked. "I couldn't believe it when I saw you." His voice was low and soft, with a husky note that gave me goose bumps.

I shouldn't have smiled so much, but I couldn't have stopped. No one else mattered. Nothing else would ever matter, I thought. Without even trying, I fell in love in an instant.

I didn't even know his name.

"This is Carey Boone," Dennis said. "And the blond is Ellie Striker. And this is Meg Floyd."

I looked at the girls, tried to fix them in my memory, and wondered if I'd even heard their names right. Their clothes were shabby and not very clean, but they wore the latest shades of lipstick and nail polish. Ellie was thin, with eyes the same color as her brother's, a curious pale brown. Meg was short and stocky, and she was working hard to smile.

"What are you doing here?" Carey asked me seriously.

"I came with my cousin," I said.

Carey's gaze flicked off Ricki and returned to me. "Why?"

The others talked, not paying attention to Carey questioning me. I shook my head helplessly. I didn't know how to answer him. At least I knew better than to tell him I'd hoped to see him again. Or that my cousin's daring was contagious.

There was a scramble while the others debated what they would do next. I wasn't surprised when Ricki won and they started off toward the Ferris wheel.

"Well, come on!" Ricki called back to Carey and me impatiently. "Catch up, Jane."

If I'd been smart, I would have paid attention to the hard stare she directed toward me.

"Do you want to ride the Ferris wheel?" Carey asked.

I shook my head. "Not particularly."

"Then let's go for a walk," he said.

I don't know if we told the others what we were going to do. We walked away, and I didn't see anything but him.

"What are you doing in Royal Bay?" he asked. He was so serious, so earnest.

"My mother and I came to get my grandmother's house ready to sell," I said. "And we're packing up her things."

He nodded. "How long are you staying?"

"Not long," I said.

He looked sober, but then he smiled suddenly. "When I first saw you a couple of days ago, I thought I knew you for a minute."

I looked down at my scuffed sneakers, speechless with delight.

He told me that he and his mother had moved to Royal Bay when he was in seventh grade. The town didn't have a high school, so he and the other teenagers commuted to Port Shasta. He was on the track team and worked on the school newspaper.

I told him about my school and my best friend. "We play in the orchestra," I said. "We're going to music camp later this summer."

"What instrument do you play?" he asked.

"Violin," I said. I wondered if he, like my cousin, would think I was boring.

He took my left hand and examined the tips of my fingers. I felt a thrill all the way to the base of my spine. "You've got short fingernails and calluses," he said. "I can tell you've been a musician for a long time." He smiled again as he let go of my hand. "Does music make you happy?"

I nodded.

"Poetry, too, I bet."

I nodded again.

He named the poets he liked best, Hopkins, Yeats, and Mary

Oliver. I wasn't surprised that they were some of my favorites, too. We liked old movies, the same kind of books.

"My favorite—this year, anyway—is *Ishmael*," he said. "Have you read it?"

"No," I said. "But I saw a copy when I was packing my grandmother's books. It didn't look as if anyone had even opened the cover. I'll take it back out of the box."

"You might like it," he said.

Oh, yes, I thought. I'd probably love his favorite book.

I couldn't understand why he had friends like Dennis and Pete. Neither of them seemed like the type who would read anything willingly or enjoy a black-and-white movie.

He didn't belong here, in the amusement park. Or in Royal Bay, either. I didn't know where he belonged. He was different, as out of place as a young eagle in a shopping mall.

Ricki and her new friends caught up with us. Ricki babbled at Carey and me, but I didn't listen. I had looked at my watch, and I was shocked at the time.

"We have to go home." I had a nightmare vision of Mom waiting for me on the porch. I looked up at Carey, hoping he didn't suspect that I had sneaked out of the house. It seemed so cheap. But he smiled.

"I don't have to go anywhere, Cinderella," Ricki said.

Her new friends snickered. Ellie's pale brown eyes met her brother's. Meg covered her mouth, and I saw that her nails were bitten to the quick. Dennis stared openly at me.

"Ricki, come on," I said. "We have to leave."

Her dark eyes snapped. "Okay, if you're afraid you'll turn into a pumpkin," she said.

"We'll come back tomorrow night," I told Carey, hoping it was true. Hoping he'd care. "I'll start reading the book."

"I'll be here, waiting to hear what you think about it," he said.

Ricki and I said good-bye to the others, and I hurried toward the gate, with Ricki lagging stubbornly behind, dawdling to look at every ride, humming under her breath, doing her best to punish me for wanting to leave.

I would have been angry with her for making things hard, if I hadn't been thinking about Carey. I was already eager for tomorrow night to come.

Chapter Three

The next morning I woke up late, past eight o'clock, with sunlight reflecting off the pale walls and filling the bedroom with warm light. The house was quiet, but I knew Mom would be up. She was always the first one up.

With a guilty conscience for company, I slid out of bed, quietly gathered together the clothes I'd planned to wear, and crept out of the room. As I hurried around the corner to the bathroom, I wondered why I'd let Ricki go on sleeping. This was the morning we were taking on the attic.

I spent only fifteen minutes showering, toweling my hair dry, and dressing, so it didn't surprise me that Ricki was still an unmoving lump in her bed.

"Hey, Ricki, time to get up," I said as I dug through my tote bag, looking for a clip for my hair.

She didn't answer.

I found the clip. "Ricki? Come on, we've got lots to do today."

She groaned but didn't move.

I fastened my hair away from my face, checked my reflection in the mirror, and said, "Ricki, get up. The sooner we eat breakfast, the sooner we can get started on the attic."

"In a minute," she mumbled. She still didn't move.

I gave up. Out in the hall, I didn't hear anything from the room my mother shared with Aunt Norma either. Could it be that she was already downstairs with Mom? I doubted it.

I found Mom standing at the sink, finishing a cup of coffee and looking out the window. Does she know? I thought in a panic. Has she discovered that I sneaked out with Ricki last night? What can I say if she's angry?

"Sorry I slept in," I said as I helped myself to cereal and milk. I couldn't look straight at her. "Ricki said she'd be up in a minute."

"Norma's still sleeping," Mom said as she rinsed her cup. "But you and I can get started in the attic. I'd like to go through the boxes, to make sure there's nothing we want. The woman from the auction house is coming today."

"Today?" I asked. I was so relieved that she didn't know what I'd done the night before that my knees nearly gave way. "Gosh, I thought we'd have more time. What about the things in the bedrooms?"

"The bedroom furniture is in good shape. We'll go through the closets, and then we'll be ready."

"Ready for what?" Aunt Norma, in a thin silk robe, trailed in. She looked around the kitchen and muttered, "I can't get over Mother spending so much money on a new kitchen. What a waste.

Was it your idea? Oh, right, you said you hadn't been here for years. If she'd asked me, I'd have told her not to spend a nickel on the place."

Mom ignored the last of Aunt Norma's whining. "Mrs. Soriano from the auction house in Port Shasta is coming today to look around once more before she makes a firm offer."

Aunt Norma pulled a chair away from the table, scraping it on the floor, and sat down. "Can somebody get me some coffee? Why did you pick her? Isn't there someone here who buys old furniture? What about Seattle? Wouldn't you get a better price from someone in Seattle who actually knows something?"

To my disgust, Mom poured coffee in a mug for Aunt Norma. It was almost automatic, as if she had waited on her sister before. "I didn't pick her, Norma. Remember? The court appointed someone who picked her, and I'm sure she's a good choice."

"Mrs. Soriano," Aunt Norma said, scowling. "Mrs. Soriano. My friends warned me to be careful about being cheated. Why are you rushing into everything?"

"You told us that you wanted all this settled before you got married . . ." Mom began.

I stared at Aunt Norma. She was getting married *again*?

She saw me staring, laughed, and fluttered her fingers. Her four diamond rings glittered. There was one for each failed marriage. "I haven't decided anything yet," she told Mom. "I always wait to see what kind of ring the man's going to give me before I promise anything."

I blinked. Did the men know that?

"Both of us want this settled and over with," Mom said in an even tone as she wiped her cup dry with a paper towel. "Right now, let's get started on the attic. Mother left several boxes there, and we should go through them."

Aunt Norma raised her eyebrows. "You're joking. I'm not going near that attic. Mother knew about my allergies, but she always made me clean up there, even though it made me sick. I won't do it this time. No, I won't. I'd be in the hospital before dinner."

Mom raised one hand to her forehead and dropped it again. "I'm sorry. I forgot your allergies. Maybe you can help out with the bedrooms then, and Ricki can work in the attic with Jane and me."

"Ricki's only a baby!" Aunt Norma squawked, sounding like an outraged hen. "And she's got a bad back, too. She was hurt trying out for the cheerleading squad last year, and she's never been the same since. The doctor says she may be in pain for the rest of her life. I only brought her with me so she could pick out a keepsake to remember her grandmother by, not to slave away in a dirty old attic."

I was dumbfounded. If Ricki was in any kind of pain, she certainly was good at keeping it a secret.

Mom didn't argue. I wished she would stick up for herself more. Her face was pale, and I wondered if she was getting one of her bad headaches again. Ever since Grandmother died, Mom had been troubled with them. I opened my mouth to ask her if her medication was up in her room, but then I changed my mind. Something warned me not to let Aunt Norma know.

Mom and I went up to the attic, and after a few minutes, I got over being so angry. We opened the windows at both ends of the big, dusty space, and let the warm wind blow through. Above the house, seagulls dipped and called. The view of Puget Sound was beautiful. Maybe somewhere out there Carey was looking at the Sound, too. And thinking about me.

The attic wasn't spooky, in spite of the cobwebs and the smell of mice and old wood. Grandmother hadn't used much of the space for storage. There were no mysterious trunks or wardrobes with ghosts in them. The boxes were neatly stacked, but not labeled. I opened one and found nothing more interesting than folded sheets.

Mom was kneeling by a small wooden chest, and she sat back on her heels to look around. "Thank goodness Mother didn't hang on to things," she said. "We should get through these boxes by lunchtime. Maybe we'll find the missing china . . ."

"What china?" Aunt Norma demanded from the stairs. "Did you find those pieces? I want them. Mother always said I was to have that set."

"Norma, I'm not arguing about it," Mom said patiently. "You can take it."

"Are you calling me selfish?" Aunt Norma said as she climbed the stairs. She was making a great show of holding a tissue over her nose and mouth.

I couldn't stand listening to her. Especially, I couldn't stand listening to Mom trying to soothe her. "I'm going downstairs for a drink of water, Mom," I said, and I brushed past Norma.

"Careful!" Aunt Norma said, shrinking back. "You'll get me dirty."

I ran down the steps and into the second floor bathroom. Slamming the door would have made me feel a little better, but I was my mother's daughter, and I didn't give in to impulses like that. I washed the dust off my face and hands, and brushed helplessly at my soiled T-shirt.

Ricki appeared in the open bathroom door. "Are you going to be in here all day?" she asked. She yawned and came in, looked around, and pulled a towel off the rack. "Boy, did I sleep," she said as she rubbed yesterday's makeup off on the clean white towel. She yawned again. "What's for breakfast?"

"Breakfast is over," I said. "It's time for lunch."

Ricki dropped the towel on the floor. "Well, you don't have to be snotty about it," she said. "What did *I* do?"

"Absolutely nothing," I said.

I was angry all over again, and started for the door before I was tempted to say anything else.

"Did your mother find out about last night?" she asked, and then she giggled. "Is that why you're so crabby?"

I whirled around. Her smile was malicious, but just as I realized that, her expression changed, and the smile became a child's, innocent and open.

"No, I don't think so," I said.

"Good," Ricki said. "Then we can go again tonight."

Something in me soared at the thought, at the same moment I understood that I had just been manipulated out of my anger.

In spite of my resentment, I was impressed with her skill.

As things turned out, Ricki and her mother went out to lunch and didn't come back. Mom and I shared a peanut butter sandwich and a can of pop in the kitchen.

In the attic, Mom had found a small box filled with old-fashioned jewelry and trinkets, and she brought it down so I could look through it while we ate.

"If you see something you like, take it," she said.

"You mean you're letting me pick something before Ricki has a chance?" I asked, laughing. "Aunt Norma won't like that."

"Norma's simply awful, isn't she?" Mom said. "I'd hoped she and Rhonda—I mean Ricki—would be of some help, but I don't think that's going to happen."

"Why do you put up with Aunt Norma?" I asked.

"I have to be careful around her," Mom said. "Does anything in the box interest you?"

"This, maybe." I put aside a small silver bracelet and held up a string of white beads. "When does the real estate agent put up the 'For Sale' sign?"

"We haven't agreed on that, either," Mom said. "Norma doesn't like the one the executor chose, so she wants someone from Seattle to come out. She says her friends told her not to trust small-town agents."

"She grew up here, too," I reminded Mom. "Maybe she knows something." I held up a moonstone earring and the light from the window caused it to gleam mysteriously. "Wow," I said.

Mom took it from me. "That's mine," she said, with wonder in her voice. "Heavens, I haven't thought about it for years. Isn't it beautiful?"

"Where's the other one?" I asked as I dumped the contents of the box out on the table. "It's got to be in here."

"No, it was lost," Mom said. She rubbed the silver around the moonstone with a paper napkin. "Well, not exactly lost, but it's gone forever."

I looked up at her with interest. "That sounds mysterious. What happened?"

"A boy gave the earrings to me," she said. She looked out the window and blinked against the brightness. "For my sixteenth birthday. Then . . ."

The doorbell rang.

Mom put the earring down and went to the front door. I heard her talking to someone, but I was more interested in the earring. I was wearing plain gold hoops, but I took one out and put on the moonstone, then hurried to the mirror over the dining room buffet to see how it looked. It needed polishing, but I could do that with toothpaste. If only I could find the other one.

I was still admiring the moonstone in the mirror when Mom came into the room with a tall, heavy-set woman with dark hair coiled in a bun on her neck.

Mom introduced me to Mrs. Soriano.

"I was just explaining to your mother that I've got a chance to bid on a private library," the woman said. "But only if I look the books over this afternoon, so I thought I'd drop by your house now."

I was glad that Aunt Norma wasn't there. I had a hunch she'd hate the confident Mrs. Soriano even more than she had thought she would.

Mom took Mrs. Soriano around the house and all the way up to the attic, while I waited in the kitchen, munching cookies. Through the window I saw an old white cat sunning itself in a far corner of the back yard. Several worried sparrows watched the cat from the trees.

When Mom finally came back to the kitchen, she was holding an envelope. "Well, she's gone. She's still pleased with everything, and she's made a formal offer. I told her I'd show it to Norma."

"You always said Aunt Norma needs money," I said. "Let's hope she's satisfied."

Mom didn't respond. I saw her take one of her headache pills with a drink of water.

I found *Ishmael* in one of the boxes stacked in the living room, and I carried the book upstairs. I'd intended only glancing at it, but it intrigued me from the first page, and I read until Mom came to find me.

Aunt Norma and Ricki still weren't back by dinnertime, so Mom and I went to the restaurant where Owen and his mother worked.

Mrs. Norris showed us to a table by the window. "We've got a fantastic beef and noodle dish tonight," she said. "You can't go wrong."

Owen appeared behind her, making desperate faces and shaking his head. When his mother left with our orders—both of us wanted the beef and noodles—Owen handed me a pink carnation exactly like the ones in the vase on our table. The flower might have been romantic if he hadn't stolen it from another table. He was fun, but he was such a *kid*.

"A glass of water and a piece of dry toast would have been a better choice," Owen said sincerely. "My dad came over to visit us, and he tried the noodles about an hour ago. He's lying down in back."

"I had a young man just like you in one of my classes this year," Mom told him as she laughed.

Owen clapped his hand to his forehead and staggered backward. "You're a teacher?" He glared at me. "Shouldn't you warn people? I thought we were going out tonight, but I'll have to rethink the whole thing now."

I shook my head, grinning. "I don't remember anything about a date," I said. "And I'm afraid I'm busy."

He slid into the seat next to me. "Busy doing what?" he asked.

"Busy helping me go through some closets," Mom said.

"Say no more," Owen said. He got up hastily. "I never interfere with people who poke around in closets."

His mother shouted something at him and he hurried away.

"I thought you might need rescuing," Mom said. "You had a trapped expression on your face. Don't you like him?"

"Sure," I said. "But not enough to go out with him. Not yet, at least."

I was thinking about Carey. Would I ever be able to tell Mom about him? She'd want to know where and when I'd met him.

I couldn't even imagine how angry she would be if she learned I had met him—no, *picked him up*—in a sleazy amusement park, after sneaking out of the house. She would never trust me again.

Why should she? I wasn't sorry, and I knew I'd do it all over again. Realizing that made me uncomfortable. Here I was, keeping secrets about a gorgeous stranger I'd met in the wrong way, while Mom obviously hoped I'd show interest in a friendly pup I'd met in the right way.

While we waited for our food, Mom used the pay phone to call Dad. I watched while the tense expression she'd been wearing all day smoothed away and was finally replaced with a grin. When she came back to the table, she said, "Your father says if we ever abandon him with the cat again, he's leaving the country."

"What happened?" I asked. Henry, our cat, liked to tease Dad.

"They had an argument over a slice of pizza," Mom said.

"Dad isn't supposed to eat pizza," I said.

"Pizza?" Owen cried as he put down our salads. "But you said you wanted noodles! My uncle is cooking a whole pot of them!"

He leaned close to me. "I know a great pizza place," he said. "Sound good? It's in Oregon. I get my driver's license on July 22, so we could . . ."

"Owen!" his mother shouted. "Let that poor child alone!"

"I'm leaving her, I'm leaving her!" Owen called back cheerfully.

He winked at Mom and she burst out laughing.

She liked Owen.

What would she think of Carey?

Guilt spoiled my appetite.

Chapter Four

Aunt Norma and Ricki were at the house when we got back. They'd had their dinner, too, in Port Shasta, where they'd spent the day shopping.

Aunt Norma had flung herself down on the sofa in the living room and kicked off her shoes. She was surrounded by shopping bags, loose sheets of tissue paper, and a tangle of colorful new garments.

"Ricki's upstairs, trying on clothes," Aunt Norma told me. "My baby loves to shop. Do the girls here all dress like you, Jane?" She wasn't smiling,

I knew my clothes weren't as exciting as hers and Ricki's, but I thought her remark was rude, so I started for the stairs. Behind me, Mom changed the subject and said, "Mrs. Soriano gave me a bid today, Norma. I think you'll be pleased. She can move most of the furniture out by Friday, and leave us beds and chairs until we're done . . ."

"I won't have it," Aunt Norma said. "I won't have somebody

taking things out while I'm here. It's not as if I can stay very long. You can bet that the minute my back was turned, Ruby Bennet made a play for my Milt. She couldn't wait to get her claws into him."

Suddenly she looked much older, and even more tired than I felt. She was upset about what her boyfriend might do when she was gone? I'd thought only teenagers worried about things like that.

"Have you tried calling him?" Mom asked gently.

"Oh, you just don't understand anything!" Aunt Norma cried. "You never did."

If I'd felt even a hint of pity for my aunt, it vanished when she spoke to Mom that way.

Why did Mom take it? Why did she have to be "careful" around her sister?

I was relieved when I reached my bedroom and could shut out their voices by closing the door.

Ricki stood before the mirror wearing white shorts, a tight yellow T-shirt, and a denim hat. "What do you think about these shorts?" she asked.

"They're fine," I said wearily.

"I wonder what those boys will think," she said as she tossed the hat on her bed. She nibbled the long nail on her forefinger, then stopped and examined the polish for a moment. "I mean Dennis and Pete . . . and Carey, of course," she added. "We'll leave as soon as Norma and Aunt Abby turn in. Are they arguing again?"

I nodded. I'll see *him* again! I thought.

"Good. They'll keep it up until they're worn out. Norma always does that to people. We can get out as soon as they come upstairs, because they'll be at it for another hour."

I glanced at my watch. "It's early yet," I said nervously.

"I'll hurry everything along," she said. She pulled her pajamas on over her shorts and shirt, then ran downstairs.

I followed her partway, and listened, amazed, to her noisy complaining. "Hey, you guys, I'm cold and worn out and I want to go to bed," she cried. "Honestly, Norma, who can sleep through all this racket? Can't you and Aunt Abby finish your fight tomorrow morning?"

Before she was done, both mothers apologized to her. She was good at what she did. Oh, yes, she was.

When Ricki and I reached the amusement park, Carey was the first person we saw. He was alone, inside the gate, watching the Devil's Loop whirling while the people in the seats screamed in fear and delight. He wore jeans and a gray knit shirt under a dark blue windbreaker. My mouth went dry.

"There's Carey," Ricki said. "He's gorgeous, isn't he? But he's awfully quiet. Don't you think he's too quiet, Jane? How do my shorts look? Is my hair okay?"

I followed along behind her, feeling clumsy and badly dressed, in spite of my neat light blue cotton slacks and my favorite white jacket. I wore the moonstone earring, too, even though I didn't have the mate. In my other ear, I wore a plain silver stud, one of a pair from the box in the attic. I'd cleaned both with a polishing cloth I found in the bottom of the box.

"Hey," Carey said when he saw us. "Hey, Jane." He smiled that smile, the one that transformed his lean, sober face. Then, politely, he dragged his gaze away from my eyes and smiled at Ricki. There was only a second when he seemed reluctant to look anywhere but at me, but that second filled me with delight.

"Where is everybody?" Ricki asked, as if the other four kids we'd met the night before were her lifelong friends. She looked around brightly, dancing a little on her high-heeled sandals, jingling her bracelets. "They aren't playing those dumb video games again, are they?"

"Pete and Dennis are," Carey said. "The girls were riding the carousel." He looked in the direction of the carousel, but there were too many people between it and the place where we stood, so he shrugged. "Maybe they moved on to something else."

Ricki gave him her most dazzling smile and then clacked away across the asphalt toward the building where the video games crouched in rows. Her wonderfully tanned arms, legs, and part of her stomach were bare, but she didn't have a goose bump on her anywhere.

Carey watched her go. "You'd think she'd freeze, dressed like that," he said, laughing and shaking his head.

Then he turned to me. "I like your earring."

I touched the moonstone with my fingers. "It belonged to my mother," I said. "She lost the other one."

He bent over me soberly and studied my earring. "My mother has an antique store here in Royal Bay. She's got boxes and boxes of old jewelry in the storeroom. Most of it isn't worth much, but I could see if she's got a moonstone like that one."

"I saw you standing outside an antique store," I said. "That was on the day we got here."

He looked straight into my eyes. "I remember. You were going by in a car. I knew I'd never seen you before, but it seemed as if maybe I had. Do you know what I mean? I got that funny feeling . . . I sound stupid, don't I?"

I hugged myself, more pleased than I was ready to admit. "You sound fine to me," I said.

The truth was that no boy had ever reacted to me in such a way. That was a thought I didn't dare explore too much, because somewhere in it I might find that *my* attraction to *him* might be partly simple gratitude. I'd never seen a boy as good-looking as Carey. That he'd stare and smile at pale, unexciting Jane was unbelievable. He had bewitched me.

He looked around the amusement park. "Would you like to ride on something?"

"Not on anything crazy," I said. I glanced over at the Devil's Loop and shook my head. "Never on that."

"The carousel? The Ferris wheel?" he asked.

"We could just walk around and watch other people," I said.

He grinned. "My favorite thing," he said.

He didn't touch me, but I felt as if he had. My whole body tingled.

We followed the path from the Loop to the arcade. "You got home all right last night?" Carey asked. "I wondered . . ."

"Of course," I said. "I'm staying in that big house . . ." I almost finished the sentence by saying, "that you pass by every night on your way here." Instead, I said, "The big house that overlooks the beach south of here. It's got an iron fence."

"I know that place," he said. "We go past it when we come here."

"Do you live nearby?" I asked.

"No, I live in the house behind my mother's shop. Ellie and Pete live on Alder Street—that's on the other side of the hill. We meet there when we're coming to the park. There's not a lot to do here."

"I started reading *Ishmael*," I told him.

"Do you like it?" he asked.

I nodded. "It's mysterious—and wonderful," I said. Like you, I added to myself. Like a silver moonstone.

"I wrote an article about it for the school paper," he said. "Some of the kids checked the book out of the library."

"Ellie and Meg?" I asked.

"Meg read it," he said. "Ellie said she'd wait for the movie."

Both of us laughed. Neither of us mentioned Pete or Dennis.

"If you don't come here at night, then where do you go?" I asked. I wasn't certain I wanted to know the answer.

He shrugged. "It's a pretty quiet town, except in summer."

I know he would have said more, but Ricki caught up with us, playfully pulling clumsy, heavy Meg behind her. "Look who I found, riding the carousel all by herself."

"Hi, Jane," Meg said. "I'm glad you came back." Her dark hair was unruly, her jeans dirty, but her smile made up for everything. She could have been a slightly grubby angel. "Did you get something to drink, Carey?"

"No, I forgot," he said. "I saw Jane coming in the gate."

Meg's smile didn't fade, but I could tell he had hurt her feelings. She was more vulnerable than the other girl, Ellie. "I'm thirsty, so I could pick something up for you," she told him. "You and Jane."

He shook his head. "We'll get something later," he said.

He was excluding her, and Ricki, too.

Ricki's eyes hardened for a moment, but then she said, "Come on, Meg, let's find Ellie and the boys. We can catch up with Jane and Carey later, and we'll all have a snack together."

I saw Meg and Carey both nod, and once again I was impressed with Ricki's ability to arrange things. But it wasn't going to be possible for Carey and me to walk around alone, because we saw Dennis and Pete running toward us.

"Hey, everybody," Dennis said, and his smile was easy and included everyone. He punched Carey's arm lightly. "I thought you were going to beat the socks off me tonight. I just cleaned Pete out."

"I thought *you* weren't going to bet real money anymore," Meg said sharply. She was glaring at Pete, not Carey. "You promised your sister that you wouldn't."

"Butt out, Meg," Pete said. He scowled and his pale brown eyes darted around as if he wanted to find someone to yell at but didn't dare.

Dennis rocked on his feet in that intense, jittery way he had. "Hey, pal, when did I ever leave you broke?" he said. He dug into his pocket and pulled out several crumpled dollar bills. "Here. You know the rules. All the money goes back to the guy that brought it."

Pete laughed harshly. "When did you make that rule up?" He didn't reach for the money. I could see both pride and anger on his face.

There was an electric moment when tension flickered among us. I felt it in my spine, felt it touch my arms, my scalp.

"Let's everybody start all over and say we didn't," Meg said. She laughed, grabbed the money out of Dennis's hand, and gave it to Pete. "Now you have to buy me a hot dog and something boiling hot to drink, Pete. The wind off the Sound is really cold tonight. Come on, everybody. We'll probably see Ellie along the way."

Meg walked with Pete, chattering constantly at him, placating him. I was reminded uncomfortably of my mother and Aunt Norma. Did Meg have to be "careful" around Pete, the way Mom said she had to be around my aunt?

Pete clearly wasn't listening. He carried the dollar bills crumpled up in his fist.

Ricki danced along beside Dennis, talking first about Los Angeles and then complaining about the wind. She still didn't have goose bumps, but Dennis took off his windbreaker and put it around her shoulders. Ricki batted her eyelashes, and Dennis smiled.

Ellie appeared out of a dark place when we passed the roller coaster. Her face was pale, and her odd tan eyes avoided mine. Without speaking, she fell into step with Carey.

"We're getting something to eat," Carey said to her.

"Sure," she said indifferently. "Are you walking home with us tonight?"

She probably went home the same way she came, along the beach, up the hill, and around my grandmother's fence.

He hesitated a moment, then said, "I don't think so, Ellie."

"But . . ." she began, then stopped.

My presence had changed his mind about something she had planned, and she was upset. But maybe he wouldn't be walking home with me, either, so I would be as disappointed as Ellie.

We bought hot dogs and hot chocolate at the outdoor cafe in the center of the park, and Meg hurried ahead to save a table for us. Most of them were filled with people hunched inside their jackets, their hands folded around steaming paper cups.

The wind off the Sound was blowing harder now. It smelled of salt water and rain, and carried with it sounds I knew were there but couldn't hear clearly because of the carousel music, so bright and false.

The amusement park was such a cheap and ugly place up close, rundown and filled with people who looked vaguely sinister. From the window in my grandmother's house, it looked magical, but that was an illusion.

Suddenly I was frightened. When I realized that I was the last one to step up to the condiment counter for mustard and relish, I wanted to drop my hot dog and run home.

"Bad night," Ellie said at my elbow as she rewrapped her hot dog in its paper napkin. She stalked away without waiting for my response.

The remaining empty seat was at the end of the table, next to Dennis. His welcoming grin gave me the feeling that he had maneuvered this—or had been persuaded to think that he had. Carey sat between Ricki and Ellie, and his unsettling silver gaze found me. Ricki chattered at him on his left, while on the other side, Ellie whispered to him behind her hand. I wondered if he heard either of them.

"So, you're from Seattle," Dennis said. His gaze was too intense. He didn't blink. His face was so close that I could have counted his freckles, and I didn't want to. "Seattle's a great place. I like it."

My mouth was full of hot dog and both of us had to wait until I swallowed.

"Yes," I said. I felt like an idiot. After the wait, I should have had something profound to say, such as, "Why do you want to sit beside me instead of Ricki?"

"You like late-night dates?" he asked.

I gawked at him. Was that some sort of insult? I had no idea how to take the question, or whether I should try to answer it.

Pete, across from me, said, "Dennis, did you see those guys hanging around the gallery? I'm sure they're from Seattle. Basketball players, maybe."

Dennis shrugged without speaking. He watched me.

"One of them was looking me over, like he recognized me or wanted to start something," Pete said, his voice raised.

"So?" Dennis said impatiently. "Let him look."

I sensed that Pete was asking permission for something and Dennis had just turned him down. Suddenly, I wanted to go home. I couldn't have explained my feelings, but those kids weren't my sort of friends—except for Carey. He would fit in anywhere. But the others, with their sidelong looks and quirked smiles, their long-standing and tangled relationships that I couldn't understand, worried me.

Ricki had finished eating, so I called out her name, but I failed to get her attention. Finally, on the third try, she looked down the table at me.

"We should leave pretty soon," I said.

"No way," she said. She laughed and whispered something to Carey, but his expression didn't change. He was watching me. Ricki saw that, too. Her smile disappeared.

I picked up my unfinished food and got to my feet. Who cares what Ricki thinks? I asked myself. I had to get away. I tossed my food into a trash can and turned to face the table.

"Time for me to leave," I told them all. I didn't meet Carey's gaze. I started off, praying that Carey would follow me and walk me home. He and I didn't belong with the others. He didn't belong in this town. Carey was as misplaced as I was among the garish rides and scruffy people.

Meg called out good-bye, Ellie ignored me pointedly, and Dennis and Pete simply stared.

Carey got to his feet. "I'll walk with you," he said.

Ricki jumped up, too. "Oh, all right, crybaby Jane. Come on, everybody. Walk up the beach with us before Janie starts to bawl."

I didn't think anyone would come, but they all did. We wandered toward the gate in an untidy bunch, bumping into each other and laughing awkwardly. I was humiliated and furious with myself for letting Ricki control everything.

As we passed the arcade, two tall boys stepped out. One glanced at Pete, muttered something to the other one, and laughed.

Instantly Pete jumped forward and shoved the boy hard, almost knocking him off his feet. But the other boy recovered, catlike in spite of his size, and hit Pete. Pete doubled up, and the boy would have hit him again, but Carey stepped between them, holding up his hands in a pacifying gesture.

"Let's not do this," he said. "We're leaving anyway. Let's keep out of each other's way."

I held my breath. Beside me, Dennis made a brief, angry sound. I reached out and touched his arm, meaning it as a warning, but he took it for something else. He moved a little, so that he stood slightly ahead of me, as if he wanted to block anyone from getting too close to me. I didn't want his protection!

The tall boys returned to the arcade without speaking. Ellie laughed nervously and said, "Dad would kill you if you got into another fight, Pete."

"Let's go," Pete said, and he jogged toward the gate without looking back. Ellie hurried after her brother.

Meg looked up at Carey as she savaged her fingernails. "Walk home with Dennis and me?" she asked him. "Those boys . . ."

He glanced at me. I didn't know what to do or say, so I averted my eyes.

"Okay, Meg," Carey said. "Unless Jane and Ricki want company on the beach. Pete and Ellie are out of sight already."

"We're fine," I blurted without thinking, and before Ricki could answer for us.

So we ended up walking home alone anyway. I should have left the arranging to my cousin, I thought. She was much better at it.

"Well, you certainly screwed that up," Ricki said as we stumbled along in the dark.

"I guess," I said.

"We could have had Carey with us if you'd played it right," she said. "Meg could have walked with Dennis."

"I think she was afraid of those other boys," I said.

"Oh, who cares about her?" Ricki said. "Carey's the prize."

I stared at her in the dark. "You spent a lot of time with Dennis and Pete," I said.

She giggled. "Well, Dennis is interesting, isn't he? Sort of a thug. Dangerous."

"You mean Pete," I said. "He was the one who was fighting."

"I know who I mean," she said. "I'm talking about Dennis. He's their leader. He's the boss of all the kids around here, I bet. Except for Carey. I haven't figured it out yet, but Carey's different."

He was. I knew that, but I didn't know why. He stood on the outside watching, but he cared about what was going on inside. It was as if he was forever an onlooker, but one who was respected so much that what he did and said mattered to the others.

I had wanted to be all alone on the beach with him. I had wanted to climb the path with him. I had wanted to say good-bye to him in the woods, so my mother wouldn't see.

The really strange part of all this was that I knew she would like him if she met him.

Unless she found out that I'd been sneaking out to see him. Why hadn't I asked Carey if we could see each other during the day, somewhere in town? I might invent a story around such a meeting, one that Mom would accept.

But I'd never asked a boy to meet me anywhere, and I knew I wouldn't find the courage to ask Carey.

As I followed Ricki up the hill, I saw that she was still wearing Dennis's jacket. I caught at the back of it and stopped her.

"The jacket," I said. "You'd better not wear it into the house, just in case we get caught. You don't want our mothers to know that we've been meeting boys."

She smiled a sharp little smile. "Oh, don't I? Don't bet on it, Janie. Don't you bet on anything."

I wasn't sure whether she wanted to get me in trouble, or just herself. Maybe the things she did were part of an ongoing battle between her and Aunt Norma. Maybe she liked goading her mother. It would be hard, having a mother who had been married four times and was about to try it again. It would be embarrassing.

But Ricki took the jacket off before we reached the gate, rolled it up and shoved it under the laurel hedge.

What game was she playing?

What game was *I* playing?

Chapter Five

I woke in the morning with a start, uncertain about where I was, and half-frightened, too. Aunt Norma was downstairs, shouting at Mom. "What does it take to get through to you?" she cried. "Don't you understand anything about money?"

I got up and pulled on my robe. Ricki didn't open her eyes or show in any way that she'd heard. I supposed that she was accustomed to her mother's yelling.

Downstairs, Mom was mixing frozen orange juice in a jug. Her cheeks were scarlet. Aunt Norma, blowsy in her soiled silk robe, sat at the table tapping her fingers.

"Mom?" I asked tentatively. "Is everything okay?"

"Sure," Mom said in a strained voice. "Is cereal all right, Jane?"

"Cereal's fine," I said. I pulled a chair away from the table and sat down. Aunt Norma stared defiantly at me. I stared back.

"Your mother refuses to learn the first thing about finances. She wouldn't spend the money to have the phone service restored, but she'll let that Soriano woman rob us. I knew I was making a mistake, going along with that judge."

"You didn't have a choice," I said angrily. "Dad told me all about it." Actually, he hadn't. And I'd avoided asking questions for two years. Nobody wants to hear too much about their parents' legal problems.

"Jane," Mom said flatly. "Never mind."

Aunt Norma picked at yesterday's dried and flaking makeup. I saw that she was eyeing the moonstone earring, which I had forgotten to take out when I had gone to bed. Suddenly she jumped up and rushed out of the room.

"Oh, great," Mom sighed.

"Sorry," I said. "I shouldn't have said anything. But it makes me mad, the way she talks to you. What's wrong *this* time?"

"She says she's going to call her lawyer and try to stop the estate from being settled again. But I don't think she can." She pressed her fingers to her temples and took a deep breath.

"You aren't getting another headache, are you?" I asked.

"I'm fine," Mom said. She put a bowl and spoon down before me. "Maybe Norma's right about keeping everything until we've finished getting the house ready. Otherwise, we'd be uncomfortable. But what would you think about moving into one of the motels?"

I shrugged, pretending indifference as my mind was busy with the problems a motel could cause. If Mom and I shared a room, I couldn't sneak out to see Carey. If Ricki and I did, then I might be able to manage it. But it would be cruel to stick Mom with Aunt Norma.

Mom sighed. "Of course, I'll be surprised if Norma and Ricki stay much longer."

My mind went blank for a moment. After last night, I could not imagine going to the park alone. It was too disturbing.

"So far, they haven't so much as made their own beds," I said. "They sure haven't helped us, not yet anyway. How long would we be here if we had to do everything ourselves?" I was too rattled to know what would serve my purpose best, Ricki in Royal Bay or Ricki back in Los Angeles.

"I had hoped we could finish everything, even the yard work, in a week," Mom said. "But the point is that Norma's supposed to pick out small things she'd like to keep, and so far all she's said she wanted is the set of china."

"Give everything to her," I said suddenly. "Let her take all the small stuff in return for staying and helping."

"She refuses," Mom said. "She still keeps saying I'm only trying to make her look bad."

"Who's looking at her?" I asked scornfully. "Who cares?" I ate breakfast, seething, while Mom wiped off the counters.

Aunt Norma shot back into the room, wearing a black caftan under a red coat and red strap sandals, and carrying a huge red bag.

"I can't sit around here doing nothing like the rest of you," she said. "I want to find a place where I can get a decent facial. I'll be back later." Her perfume, which had entered the room before her, lingered after the front door slammed.

"Let's get dressed," Mom said, as if nothing had happened. "We might as well get an early start on the day. I want to pick up more cleaning supplies and groceries."

"What about Ricki?" I asked. "Should I ask her if she wants to come?"

"Why not?" Mom said.

Asking Ricki anything in the morning was nearly impossible. I finally got her to mumble, "Umm?"

"Do you want to walk into town with us?" I asked for the fourth time.

"You must be crazy," she said. "I'm not walking anywhere this morning. Leave me alone." She rolled over so that her back was turned to me and that was that.

I looked around the bedroom with disgust. Her clothes were scattered everywhere. Every flat surface was littered with her makeup. Angrily I pulled back the curtains and gave them a good shake. Dust floated in the stream of sunlight. Ricki didn't stir.

As Mom and I left the house, the dirty white cat I had seen before fled from the front garden. The moment he left, two thrushes fluttered down to an overgrown flower bed.

"I wonder who owns that cat," I said. "He could use a bath."

"Tell that to *your* cat," Mom said with a smile. "Hey, I like seeing you wearing the moonstone earring. You should go through the box and see if there's anything else you want."

"Grandmother's silver studs," I said promptly. "But that's all, really. It will be nice, having your earring and a pair of hers. But I probably only saw Grandmother a dozen times in my whole life. I should be feeling something about being here, but I don't, so I feel—I don't know—guilty, maybe. But how about you? Is being here and going through everything hard for you?"

"No, not really," she said. I saw her biting her lower lip. "My mother was a cold person," she said vaguely.

I touched the moonstone earring. "Did she like the boy who gave you these?"

Mom shrugged. "I didn't know, I honestly didn't. Usually she was polite but uninterested in my friends."

"What about Aunt Norma?" I asked, not really caring. It was just something to say.

Mom didn't answer. I glanced over at her again. Her face was without expression, carefully guarded.

"She hated him," I guessed. "Well, I don't suppose you cared."

"She was crazy about him," Mom said suddenly, almost angrily. "She was a year older than he was, ready to leave for college, but she developed a big crush on him, and he wasn't interested in her. I think she actually scared him. Norma could be very manipulative, even when she was a teenager."

She fingered the gold hoops in her ears, as if checking to make sure she hadn't lost one.

"So what happened?" I asked.

"He gave me the moonstones on my sixteenth birthday, and Norma worked herself up into a rage about it. We'd gone to the amusement park one afternoon—I can't remember why. Neither of us particularly liked the place. She bought us tickets for the Ferris wheel, and while we had stopped at the very top so some other people could get on, we started arguing. Norma grabbed one of the earrings—she pulled the loop right out of my ear!—and threw it down into the crowd below. I got off as soon as I could, but I couldn't find it. I suppose someone picked it up."

I stared at her. "You're kidding. That was a rotten thing to do. What did the boy say?"

"I didn't tell him Norma had done it," she said. "He already thought she was impossible. I just told him I'd lost it."

"I can see why you don't like the amusement park," I said after a moment.

"It's an awful place anyway," Mom said. "I can't imagine why we went. It attracted the worst kids around, and I'll bet it still does. Besides, it's dangerous."

"Did anyone ever get hurt there?" I asked, remembering the screaming people on the Devil's Loop.

"A few times," Mom said slowly.

"Anyone you knew?" I asked.

"A friend of Norma's fell from one of the rides." Mom spoke hesitantly, as if she was having trouble recalling it.

"What happened?"

"I don't know," Mom said abruptly. "But I don't want you going to the place."

The grocery store was in sight. Mom slowed.

"I think my family troubles were too much for the boy who gave me the earrings," she said after a moment. "Whenever he came to the house, Norma was angry and slamming doors. Or saying things about him that he could hear. By the time summer was over, we weren't dating anymore. He just drifted away. I'd see him watching me at school sometimes. But nothing more happened."

I shook my head. "That's sad. He was your very first love, right?"

Mom laughed. "No, actually, he was my second. Before him, I'd had a crush on a boy named Jack. He moved away, and I sat on the sea wall every afternoon for a month, crying over him. Sorry to disappoint you."

"It's hard to think about you involved with anybody but Dad," I said.

"Well, he's a winner, isn't he?" Mom said.

In the grocery store, Mom concentrated on filling our cart. I had been too daring, questioning her about the amusement park. The conversation was over, but my hands were still clenched so hard that my nails cut into my palms. It was clear that I couldn't expect Mom to accept Carey, once she learned where I'd met him.

After we finished shopping, we stopped at a small cafe and ordered sandwiches and lemonade. We could see the marina from the windows, and watched a boat edging its careful way in.

"If this good weather continues, the tourists will start showing up early," Mom said. "I'm amazed that it's not raining."

"Was it fun here, when the tourists came?" I asked.

Mom shook her head. "I think I inherited my mother's resentment of them. Everything was nicer after summer was over. But the town needed tourists after the cannery closed."

Our lunch was good, but I could tell that Mom's headache was back, so while we were walking home, I did my best to make her feel better about everything.

"Maybe Aunt Norma will be back, and willing to help around the place," I said. "Maybe Ricki will work in the yard with me this afternoon." I had planned to weed the flower beds in front.

"Maybe," was all Mom said.

But Aunt Norma's rental car wasn't there when we got back. And Ricki was sitting in the kitchen eating bread and jam and drinking a can of pop. She was wearing a swimsuit and lots of tanning lotion.

"Did you go down to the beach?" I asked as I helped myself to pop from the refrigerator.

"That rocky old place?" she asked scornfully. "No way. I put a blanket out on the lawn in back. I have to keep working on my tan, you know. I don't want to end up looking like you, pale as a grub."

"Thanks," I said cheerfully. "I'll send you a get-well card when you get skin cancer."

"Girls," Mom said.

Ricki smirked. "How come you're so cranky?"

"I get tired doing so much of the work around here," I said. "You can work on your tan while you're helping me weed the flower beds."

Ricki rolled her eyes. "I hurt my back, remember? And I haven't been getting much sleep at night."

Her daring amazed me. But then, my own daring amazed me. I shouldn't take chances by picking quarrels with her.

"I'll help, Jane," Mom said. "We'll work outside this afternoon and tackle the second floor closets this evening. We don't need daylight for that."

Ricki's grin infuriated me, but I kept my mouth shut, even when she told us she was going upstairs for a nap. A nap! She slept more than anyone I'd ever known.

Mom pulled weeds in the long flower bed that separated Grandmother's house from the Phares'. I worked on the rose bed beside the iron fence in front. I was on my knees, digging with a trowel, when I saw the white cat again, crouching under the laurel hedge. His eyes were the color of golden coins, and he watched me without blinking.

"Hey, kitty," I said. "Come here, kitty, kitty."

Mom stood up and joined me. "Poor thing," she said. "He looks like a stray."

I had a horrible thought. "He couldn't have been Grandmother's, could he? Alone here all this time?"

"No, no, she didn't like cats," Mom said. "We never had pets. Let's see if he's friendly."

We walked slowly toward the hedge, but the cat shot away and disappeared down the path that led to the beach, and then into the woods.

"If we see him again, why don't we give him something to eat?" I said.

Mom agreed, and we went back to work. Overhead, two seagulls shrieked. The sunlight was filtered now by a thin layer of clouds.

After a while, Mom said her headache was wearing her out and she wanted a cup of tea. I worked on after she went back in the house, trying to think through my problems. If I could have kept Carey off my mind for any time at all, I might have found my common sense. As it was, I had no solution to anything, except that I wanted and needed to see more of him.

No matter what I had to do.

Chapter Six

It was after five o'clock before I was satisfied with the front yard and put the tools away in the garage. I might have worked longer, but the Phares came out and told me they were driving to Port Shasta for dinner and wouldn't be back until the next day. By the time they drove away, I'd begun noticing how sore my muscles were.

I liked yard work. It gave me a chance to think, not that I'd been doing much real thinking that afternoon. I'd been daydreaming about Carey, wondering what might happen in the short time I had left in Royal Bay. Wondering why I was feeling things about him I'd never felt about another boy. And I hardly knew him!

It was more than his looks, or his obvious attraction to me. I liked his gentle, quiet ways, his ability to bring peace to an awkward situation, and his sudden laughter. I was glad that he was polite and soft-spoken. And I knew that Kitty would like him, too.

Not that she'd ever have a chance to meet him. Face up to it, Jane, I told myself. This is one of those summer romances, no matter how much it hurts to admit it.

I found Mom in the kitchen, wiping spilled pop off the floor. "Ricki's up from her nap," she said.

"I can tell," I said as I studied the mess of tortilla chip crumbs and smeared salsa on the counter. Obviously Ricki had fixed herself a snack while Mom and I were working. "Do you suppose she'll want dinner after she porked down all this stuff? I'm starved."

"Norma's not back yet," Mom said as she straightened up, wincing.

"Well, that's too bad," I said, exasperated. "What if she doesn't show up until midnight? Come on, Mom, let's go into town and eat. Ricki can come with us if she wants, or she can stay here."

"Ricki's not staying here," my cousin chirped from the doorway. "Were you two sneaking out on me?"

"We're leaving for dinner as soon as we've had our showers," Mom said firmly. She used a different tone with Ricki, the one that she should have been using with her sister.

Ricki shrugged. "That's okay with me. I don't want anything more than salad or a dessert, but just don't leave me behind, that's all."

I wondered if she'd been left behind a lot by her mother. Ricki aggravated me sometimes, but still, I felt sorry for her.

After my shower, I put on a dress made of thin blue material, with a skirt that stopped several inches below my knees, a scoop neck, and short sleeves. I carried my white jacket, in case I got cold on the way home.

In contrast, Ricki changed to a short black shiny skirt, a silver halter top, and a red jacket. She looked me over carefully, then shrugged and smirked.

"Is that your mother's dress?" she asked. She wore a little cat smile.

I should have been angry, but I burst out laughing. "You're really awful, aren't you?" I asked.

She shrugged again. "I guess maybe I am. Does it matter?"

I had a hunch that my answer really would matter to her. "No and yes," I said. "No, because we'll be going home in a few days and who knows when we'll see each other again? But yes, because we ought to be friends, especially since we're cousins."

It was her turn to laugh. "Our mothers are sisters, and they hate each other. Haven't you noticed? Come on, Janie. I'm on to you. You're afraid to make me mad because I might tell on you."

"And I might tell on *you*," I said, doing my best to sound as if I didn't care. But she'd scared me again.

"You better be nice to me," she whispered as Mom came downstairs.

"Okay, people," Mom said. "Where shall we eat?"

Quickly, Ricki said she didn't want to eat in the restaurant where she and her mother had run into us the first night. "The one where that boy works," she added, as if I hadn't known what she meant.

"You said you weren't hungry, Ricki," Mom said. "Why should it matter that much to you if you'll only order a salad or dessert anyway?"

Ricki, scowling, shrugged that eloquent shrug of hers. "Oh, all right," she told Mom. "But I can't imagine what you see in the place."

Mom left a note for Aunt Norma, telling her where we'd be. We ended up taking the car because Ricki said she was too tired to walk, and her back was bothering her again. I wondered if lying in bed all day could cause that.

As we entered the restaurant, Owen and his mother saw us at the same time. Mrs. Norris immediately said, "Owen!" even though he hadn't had time to do anything yet.

He padded across the carpet to us. "Would you like to sit at the table right outside the kitchen door? That way you can peek in and check up on my uncle. He's had a rotten day and who knows what he's doing to the food this time?"

His mother bustled over, took him by the ear, and moved him away. "I've got a nice table by the window," she told us. "Three of you tonight? Come along, then. Ignore Owen, if you can. I'm running an ad in the classifieds and hoping to sell him before the weekend gets here."

Owen, hurrying along behind me, whispered, "I'm cheap and immediately available for anything you might have in mind. And I do mean *anything*—a movie, a nice walk in the country, a quick trip to Wilbur's Little Wedding Chapel, or if you don't like that idea, there's a tattoo parlor I know about that—"

"Owen, do you want me to tell your father that you've decided you don't need an allowance any longer?" his mother asked over her shoulder.

I laughed. But I saw that Ricki didn't. Owen didn't seem to care. I felt a mean sort of satisfaction that he wasn't any more impressed with my cousin than Carey was. She wasn't as terrific as she thought.

Between Mrs. Norris and Owen, we heard about the day's specials and ordered pepper steaks and salads. Even Ricki changed her mind and asked for a whole dinner.

"Good," Mom told her. "You need a big meal. I don't think you had much of anything except chips and pop today."

Ricki sighed. "Come on, Aunt Abby. Don't go all motherly on me. I hate that."

We didn't talk much during the meal, and Owen was busy helping—and pestering—two other groups who'd come in after us. I saw him look over at me several times, and I wondered if he knew Carey and the other kids from the amusement park. No, probably not. He was a stranger here, too. Like me, only without Ricki as an ice-breaker.

When we got home, Aunt Norma still wasn't there. I knew that Mom was beginning to worry, but Ricki didn't seem to care.

She complained because we didn't have phone service or cable TV, but finally sat down to watch one of Grandmother's old movie tapes. I tried to concentrate on it, but I was nervous, thinking about Carey again, and having trouble keeping my eyes off my watch.

I wanted to ask Ricki if we were still going to the amusement park that night. But Mom was in the dining room, going through a box of small table linens she'd found in the back of the pantry.

"Gosh, I'm tired," Ricki said suddenly, and she proved it with a huge yawn. "I'm going upstairs. If Norma comes in, tell her I got tired of waiting for her and went to bed."

I jumped up to follow her, but Mom called me into the dining room to see the old napkins she'd found. I looked down at them blindly, unable to concentrate on the hemstitching she pointed out.

Were Ricki and I going to the park this early? What if her mother came home and wanted to talk to her?

"I think Norma might like these," Mom said and she smoothed the napkins. "They'd be perfect with the set of china she's taking."

"I thought she didn't want it because some of the pieces are missing," I said.

"I'm sure she'll end up taking the set home with her. She might be able to find replacements for the missing pieces. I'll set the napkins aside and show them to her when she gets back. They're gorgeous. But I have no idea what to do with the rest of the things in the box. None of it's worth saving." She looked around, puzzled. "Did Ricki go upstairs?"

"Yes, she said she was tired," I said. My voice sounded strange to me. "She doesn't want Aunt Norma to wake her up when she comes in."

Mom didn't say anything, but folded tissue paper around the good napkins and pushed the box into a corner.

"You must be tired," I said. "Why don't you quit for the day? You could watch a video."

"No, I'd better keep going for a while longer," Mom said. "The real estate agent is coming tomorrow. Norma can meet him and who knows—the place might be on the market by tomorrow afternoon. We don't have to stay here until it's sold, thank goodness. But it would help if everything's cleared out."

Suddenly I realized that our time in Royal Bay was really running out. My stomach tied into a knot. We'd already been here four days out of the seven we'd planned. Three more days.

Three!

I touched the moonstone earring and felt something like an electric shock.

"If you don't need me for anything, I think I'll go to bed early, too," I said, hoping I sounded casual.

Before Mom had a chance to answer, the door opened, Aunt Norma came in, and the door closed with a crash. It was like being invaded by an army.

"What a stupid day!" she cried. She pulled off her coat and threw it on the sofa. "That rental car died on me three blocks from here. Can you believe it? It acted up all day, stalling on hills and at red lights. I'm lucky I wasn't stranded in the parking lot outside the beauty salon. Now it's completely dead. And the cell phone in it doesn't work, either. Why on earth didn't you have the phone connected here? Now what am I supposed to do?"

Instinctively, I backed up a step when she came into the dining room.

"There are plenty of pay phones a few blocks away," Mom said patiently. "Do you want to call the car rental place?"

"I suppose so," Aunt Norma seethed. She sat down at the table and kicked off her high-heeled shoes. "Why did I agree to come here? I hate straightening out messes. I always leave things like that to somebody else. Those rental people have got to bring me another car. This is all their fault. I want a car tonight."

Mom sighed. "I'll drive you to a phone. Or you could go next door and ask the Phares if you can use theirs."

"They aren't coming back from Port Shasta until tomorrow morning," I said.

Aunt Norma glared at me as if it was my fault that the Phares were out of town. "Well, come on then, Abby. Let's get going. Let's find a phone."

They left, and I went upstairs to tell Ricki what had happened. She wasn't in our bedroom. The bathroom was empty, too. And she wasn't in any of the other rooms on the second floor. I didn't need to look to be sure she wasn't in the attic.

I hurried to the windows and looked out. There she was, barely visible in the deepening twilight, stumbling along the rocky beach toward the amusement park.

She had sneaked out, but how she had managed it baffled me. Mom and I had been in the dining room and could see into the kitchen easily.

Except—the kitchen light had been out.

Still, we hadn't even heard the door. Ricki was amazing. And infuriating.

What if her mother had wanted to talk to her? I had a hunch she had expected me to think up an excuse for her. Like her mother, Ricki left cleaning up messes to somebody else.

Well, I couldn't follow her. There was too much of a chance that

Mom would want to check on me when she got back, even if it was only peeking in the bedroom door.

Meanwhile, Ricki was with the amusement park kids—and Carey.

I went back to the living room with *Ishmael,* and settled down to read. And I tried to look as if nothing was bothering me, in case Mom and Aunt Norma came through the door.

But I couldn't help running my hand over the page I was reading and thinking that Carey had read those same words in his own book, more than once, and he loved them. Perhaps we hadn't known each other very long, but we could say, "Remember the part in the book . . ." and know what each other meant. We had a past now, a history.

I looked at my watch again. Soon, I thought. Soon.

Chapter Seven

Mom and Aunt Norma came back ten minutes later. Aunt Norma, the first one through the door, threw her purse on the sofa and sat down hard. "They've got a lot of nerve," she said to no one in particular.

"The rental people promised you another car tomorrow," Mom said, and I could tell that she was trying hard to sound reasonable and calm. And careful. "That will work out, Norma. You really need to be here when the real estate man comes."

"Oh, for heaven's sake!" Aunt Norma said. "A real estate agent." She noticed me and stared. "Where's Ricki?"

"In bed," I lied. "She said she'd see you in the morning." I thought of trying a yawn, but knew I couldn't pull it off, especially since I was wide awake and nervous enough to be unable to sleep again for maybe the rest of my life.

Aunt Norma sighed. "Well, I suppose that's a good idea. I'm exhausted." She got up and started for the stairs without another word.

Mom looked over at me and shook her head wearily. I waited until Aunt Norma slammed the bedroom door before I said, "You look worn out, Mom."

"A long hot bath sounds good, but I'd better take it down here. I'd hate to disturb Norma, because she might not settle down again for an hour."

Something in me snapped. "Why do you tiptoe around her? Take your bath upstairs if you like. Who cares what she thinks? Why are you acting like this?"

Mom sighed. "I don't want to give her an excuse to complicate everything again," she said. "I want this mess over with. I never really imagined that she'd actually help out with the work, but if she doesn't have a chance to pick out the keepsakes she wants, she might retaliate by thinking up some new way of stalling. I'm afraid she's better at creating problems than I am at solving them."

Mom wore a new expression. She looked bitter, and the bitterness seemed oddly at home on her face, as if it had been there before and left a deep and sad impression.

"Mom . . ." I began.

She shook her head, and the expression disappeared. Now she looked a little amused. "I should call your father. Maybe he'd come and give us a hand after all."

"But if he takes his vacation now, we can't go to Canada," I said.

Mom leaned back and sighed, exhausted. "Of course. I'm sorry. For a minute, I was looking around for somebody to rescue me from my sister. All of us should solve our own problems."

"Sometimes problems get too big," I said. "Aunt Norma is pretty big."

Mom burst out laughing. "Oh, she'd love that," she said.

It was good to hear her laugh.

And why was I taking the risk of making her angry?

"Go on to bed, Jane," Mom said. "You worked awfully hard today, and tomorrow's the day we're finishing up on the closets, for sure. It won't be much longer before we're in good enough shape to put up the 'For Sale' sign and go home."

"I'll try not to wake Ricki," I said. The lie didn't stick in my throat and choke me to death the way it should have. "And I'll try really hard not to disturb Aunt Norma."

"And I'll take my long soak down here," Mom said.

From my bedroom window, I looked out at the beach. Clouds blew across the lopsided moon, so sometimes I saw nothing but the lights of the fairyland amusement park and the heaving darkness that was the Sound. I pushed open the window and heard the distant tempting music, even though I knew what the shadows hid. Unwillingly, I remembered my unease there, and how uncomfortable I was with the amusement park kids.

But Carey was there.

I heard Mom come upstairs, probably for her pajamas and robe. I waited until she went back down and had time to undress and get into the tub, and then I crept downstairs, keeping close to the wall the way my cousin taught me.

I flew through the kitchen and out the back door. Magic had touched me. I didn't make a sound.

I hurried through the open gate, and then to the path. A cloud rolled over the moon.

I felt my way carefully, and when I reached the place where the path dipped into the woods, the cloud blew away. In the light, I saw Carey—It must be him! I thought—standing at the bottom of the hill where the path gave way to the rough sand. He faced the Sound, watching the moonlit water pull and retreat, pull and retreat on the rocky beach.

"Carey," I said softly.

He turned instantly. "You're here," he said. "I was afraid you weren't coming."

"There was something I had to do," I said, lying to him as easily as I had lied to my mother, but at least I still had enough self-respect to feel uncomfortable. "Where's Ricki?"

"I don't know," he said. "At the park, I guess." He looked down at me for a long moment, then smiled suddenly, transfixing me.

"I brought you something," he said. He held out his hand.

In the moonlight, I could see another silver earring. I reached for it carefully and held it up. A moonstone dangled from a French loop.

"I found it in with some other jewelry in my mother's store-room," he said. "I'm not sure it's much like the one you have, but it's a moonstone."

"I know," I said. I removed the silver stud and put in the earring. "It doesn't matter if it doesn't match exactly. It's just wonderful to have it." I paused. "How much does it cost?"

He shook his head firmly. "It's to remember me by," he said. "When you leave."

I looked straight into his eyes, speechless.

"Moonstones look right on you," he said. "They're like you, calm and serene. Quiet, not jittery and confused. Do you know what I mean?" He took a deep breath. "I want you to remember me," he whispered. "I'm afraid you won't."

I shook my head. "Oh, don't you worry about that," I said. "I'll remember you."

At that instant, I wondered if he would kiss me. But he didn't. Instead, he smiled that incredible smile again, and glanced back over his shoulder at the fairyland. "Let's go," he said. "Let's ride on the Ferris wheel tonight."

"And talk about the book," I said. "We have things in common now, like old friends."

"Yes," he said.

We were on our way to the Ferris wheel when we saw the other kids. My first impulse was to run, but we waited for them to catch up with us, and I willed myself to smile. It was hard work. I remembered the fight the night before, and wondered what awful thing might happen next.

"I thought you weren't coming tonight, Jane," Ricki said. She was wearing Dennis's jacket again. From the smile on her face, no one would guess that she had sneaked out on me.

"I wouldn't miss it," I said.

Her smile extended to her eyes then. Oh, yes, she could count on me to cover up for her and not let anyone else know that she had deliberately left me behind. What else was I supposed to do?

I saw her gaze flick to my new earring. "Where'd you get that?" she demanded. "You only had one when I left."

I touched the earring, but I couldn't think of anything to say.

Meg and Ellie watched curiously. Ellie's head was cocked to one side as she studied first the earring and then Carey and me. Meg gnawed on her thumbnail. Dennis and Pete weren't especially interested in earrings, but I sensed that they were waiting, too. I thought that they always paused in a critical moment to see if there was a chance something more might develop. Something extreme.

I glanced over at Carey, looking for a signal. Did he want me to tell them that he had given the earring to me? Or would I embarrass him?

"I found it for her," Carey said easily. "She only had one."

"It doesn't match," Ellie said with satisfaction. Her tan eyes glinted.

"That's all right," I said. "I want to be able to tell them apart."

Ellie made a disgusted noise, and Meg elbowed her. "Come on, everybody," she said with nervous cheer. "Let's do something."

"Jane and I want to ride on the Ferris wheel," Carey said, and he closed his hand around my upper arm and turned me away from the group. It was obvious that he was trying to exclude them.

But Ellie didn't want to be excluded. And the boys wanted to be part of the group. Only Meg hung back, her cheeks pink, her eyes hurt. I saw that her fingertips were bleeding.

She liked Carey. I hadn't realized that Ellie was interested in him, too. I'd thought she cared more about Dennis.

"Well, I'm not riding on anything as silly as a Ferris wheel," Ricki said. "It's kid stuff, you guys. I'm in the mood for excitement. How about the Devil's Loop, Dennis?"

She danced in front of him, smiling, beckoning with both hands as if inviting him closer to her.

"Sounds good," he said. "But won't you be afraid, riding in that chair all by yourself?"

She shook her head. "I'm not afraid of anything," she said.

Carey looked down at me as we moved away. "Are you sure you don't want to go with them?"

I shook my head.

I looked back only once, to see Ricki walking away with Ellie, while Meg hurried along, trying to keep up with Dennis and Pete. They were talking over her head, ignoring her.

I was surprised. I would have expected to see Ricki between the two boys, pitting them against each other. That was more her style.

Ricki was complicated. If I had been smarter, I could have seen that people can hide inside a tangle of complications, and keep you off guard.

The Ferris wheel stopped when Carey and I were at the very top, and the moon was clear of clouds, silvering the beach so brightly that I thought I could count each stone. The water lay still like cold, melted metal and then rocked a little, lazily, as if nothing much mattered in moonlight. Nothing much mattered anywhere except the magic. We were too high to see how shabby the park was.

"The tide is turning," Carey said. "If we get to sit here long enough, you can see it happen."

But we moved again, sank to the bottom, and our turn was up.

We bought hot chocolate in the restaurant and carried our cups to a bench near the carousel.

"Do you like Royal Bay?" Carey asked.

"It's starting to fill up with tourists, isn't it? I see more people around every day." I had avoided answering him directly, because I wasn't ready to tell him that the only thing in Royal Bay that mattered was him.

"By July, it's crazy here," he said. "I don't like it then. I always go to Montana to stay with my dad."

Did my heart stop beating? Or did the world stop?

When I finally came alive again, I said, "When are you leaving?"

"The first of July," he said. "Dad already sent me my airline ticket."

Ricki and Dennis joined us, holding bags of popcorn. Ricki, choking on a laugh, grabbed Carey's arm and let her forehead rest against his shoulder. "Oh, that was the funniest thing I ever saw," she gasped.

"What was?" Carey asked innocently, right on cue.

"You had to be there," Ricki said, linking her arm in Dennis's. "Right, Dennis? You had to be there and see what a fool Ellie made out of herself."

She'd gone too far and knew it at the second that the expression on Dennis's face changed from amusement to rejection. Ellie was Pete's sister. Ricki was some rich girl from out of town. "I need my jacket," he told Ricki as he pushed her arm away.

"Hey, Boone," he said to Carey as he shrugged into his jacket. "You ready to take me on tonight?"

He wanted Carey to play video games, and it was a command rather than an invitation. I wondered why he didn't think of the games as kid stuff.

What would Carey do? I wondered. This was a sort of test. I felt that awful *pause* again, when everything bad in the world crouched, ready to leap.

"I'll come along when I'm finished," Carey said easily, raising his cup of hot chocolate and tasting it.

"See you, then," Dennis said coolly, and he left without saying goodbye to Ricki. I saw Meg and Ellie in the crowd outside the arcade, and tall Pete looming over everybody.

I sipped my hot chocolate, nervous and uncertain. Ricki made herself at home on the other side of Carey, chattering about nothing the way she did sometimes, apparently indifferent to Dennis's rejection. I watched the others outside the arcade and wondered about their relationships with each other.

Dennis was the leader, that I knew. Pete was angry with the world. Both girls liked Carey best, but Ellie would settle for Dennis, and poor Meg would settle for anybody who would settle for her. Ricki and I were a disturbance, pebbles dropped in their pond and making ripples. Everything had changed a little.

Or maybe a lot.

"Jane, we'd better go back," Ricki said, leaning over Carey's lap. "The later we are, the worse it will be if we get caught."

I sucked in my breath and looked at Carey.

Carey glanced quickly at her and then at me. "Get *caught?*" he asked. He shook his head in disbelief. "Doesn't anyone know you're here?"

My face burned. He wasn't surprised because I sneaked out, I suspected. Sneaking out wouldn't bother a boy. But he was surprised that I was hiding him from my mother, as if I was ashamed of him.

What was I supposed to say? Oh, please, I thought, give me a chance to think straight. I needed time to plan what I could tell my mother about how I met Carey—something that didn't involve getting picked up at an amusement park she didn't want me to go near. If I knew what to tell Mom, I could introduce Carey to her.

I should have already done that. I could have told her practically anything about meeting him, so long as it was in daylight and not in a place she hated as much as she hated the amusement park. Then I could have told him what I'd worked out . . .

And we'd be right back where we were. He'd know I was ashamed of how we'd gotten together. Why hadn't I been prepared for this?

Ricki, behind Carey's shoulder, grinned at me. "Let's go home, Jane," she said. "We want to be able to come back tomorrow night, right, Carey?"

He hesitated for just a moment, and then smiled down at me, and everything uneven and jagged was healed over.

"I'll walk back down the beach with you," he said. He leaned toward me and touched his forehead to mine. "And I'll see you tomorrow night, okay? Same time, same place?"

I suppose we talked as we walked along the beach, but I wondered what he really was thinking. And why I felt so cheap.

I hated Ricki so much at that moment that my mouth was dry and my head ached.

Chapter Eight

I didn't sleep that night. Ricki's snore—she sounded like the motor in a refrigerator—filled me with even more resentment. How could she sleep after what she had done?

A light rain began falling at daybreak, and by the time I got up, it had turned into a downpour. The room was cold and felt damp. And it was unbelievably messy.

Ricki was a pig. Every flat surface except my bed was littered with her junk—cosmetics, hair dryer, little useless purses, and tangles of belts, jewelry, and two different curling irons. All the clothes she'd worn since she arrived were scattered across the floor, along with a trashy paperback romance and a soap opera magazine.

The room smelled like her cologne, musk mixed with something eye-stinging and sharp. By then I'd learned that my cousin only showered to wash her hair, and she only washed her hair to make styling easier. She, her own self, smelled faintly like gym socks.

Ricki was disgusting and pathetic at the same time. Her mother was horrible, and along with not teaching her manners—not that Aunt Norma had any herself—apparently she hadn't given her any clues at all that there was more to grooming than plastering on another layer of makeup.

"You're mad at me, aren't you?" Ricki said from under her mound of blankets. I was surprised that she was awake.

"Don't flatter yourself," I said, doing my best to sound self-confident. "I haven't been thinking about you at all." I pulled on my robe and started for the door.

"Don't make me do something to you that you'll be sorry for," she said evenly as she sat up. Her eyes were as hard as pebbles.

"*What?*" I gasped.

"Oh, you heard me, Janie," she said. She sighed and looked appraisingly around the room. "I hate this room. I hate this whole house, just as much as my mother does. Look at the mess. But I can't pick stuff up. I can't bend over because of my back. Norma has to pick up after me, or else the housekeeper does."

"Well, I'm not doing it," I said, and I started for the door again.

"You're like your mother," she said.

I kept going. My hand was on the knob.

"You're a sneaky bitch."

Like an idiot, I stopped and looked back.

She smiled widely, satisfied that she had caught my attention.

I opened the door and escaped. I had both moonstone earrings in the pocket of my robe, and I closed my fingers around them, hoping they would bring me luck.

The kitchen was cold, too. I heated water in the microwave for tea. While I waited, I looked out the window and saw the white cat crouched on the deck, its shoulders hunched. I grabbed a small bowl from the cupboard, filled it with milk, and eased the door open. The cat shot away, but I left the milk in the shelter of the eaves.

Mom, dressed in jeans and a heavy sweatshirt, came down to the kitchen when I was halfway through my cereal. She was unusually pale. I wondered if she'd slept well. If she had been awake last night when I came in . . . *If she knew* . . .

She shook the cereal box and said, "We forgot cereal yesterday. I guess we need to go back to the grocery store."

"I wish I knew how much longer we'll be staying," I said, and I dreaded her response because I didn't know what I wanted to do, go or stay.

"The real estate agent comes this morning. If we're lucky, Norma will choose whatever she wants to keep today. Then all we have to do is arrange to have the furniture picked up and finish cleaning the place."

"Could we be leaving as soon as tomorrow?" I asked. I didn't dare look at her.

She put a cup of water in the microwave and turned it on. "Wouldn't that be wonderful?" she said. "But I don't think it's possible. Two more days should do it, if everything goes right, that is. Three days at the most. I'll be glad to get home. Royal Bay is only fun if you didn't spend your childhood here."

Before I had a chance to reply, someone rang the doorbell.

"Who on earth . . ." Mom began.

I looked at my watch. "It's not even seven-thirty."

She hurried through the house to the door while I listened. I heard her say, "It's here?" and then, "I'll call her."

She called Aunt Norma from the foot of the stairs, then went halfway up to call her again. Norma answered with an unintelligible cry, as if she had been frightened out of sleep, and I got up to see what was going on.

A young woman wearing a raincoat stood in the doorway, looking definitely unhappy. Behind her another young woman stood, waiting. I could see two small cars sitting in the driveway, one parked behind Mom's car and the other in front of the garage door.

Aunt Norma came down, pulling on her silk robe. "What?" she asked. "Who wants me at this hour?"

Mom said, "Some people from the car rental agency."

Aunt Norma shuffled to the door. "What kind of car did you bring?" she asked the woman in the raincoat. "I asked for a comfortable . . ." She looked out the door. "Are you joking? I hate small cars, and I'm certainly not driving either of those."

The young woman at the door sighed and said, "The red one is for you. Please sign here. We're having your other rental— the one you left in the middle of the street—towed away. I'm authorized to give you a discount because of the inconvenience."

Aunt Norma argued, the young woman scowled, and I went back to the kitchen, shaking my head.

Ricki was pouring the milk down the sink. "The milk's sour. Didn't you know, or don't you care?"

"It *isn't* sour," I said. "You're imagining it. We bought the milk yesterday."

"What am I going to have for breakfast?" she said.

"Your mom's new rental car is here," I said. "The two of you can drive to a restaurant, I guess."

She snickered. "Boy, you *are* mad, aren't you? Well, think how much worse it could be."

"I *can't* think how much worse it could be," I said. "All I want is to get away from you."

"Don't you wish," Ricki said. "Don't you just wish."

By the time I had showered, Ricki had gone back to bed. Downstairs, our mothers were arguing again.

"What time do the grocery stores open?" I asked Mom, deliberately interrupting my aunt in the middle of a sentence. "I'll do the shopping."

"Jefferson's opens at eight," Mom said.

"Don't go there," Aunt Norma said. "Mother always said they have terrible produce."

"That was twenty years ago," Mom began patiently. "And Jane's not getting produce." She went on, explaining and explaining, with her fingers at her temples again. I wondered why she put up with being treated that way—and why I put up with Aunt Norma myself.

"I don't want Jane to go there," Aunt Norma said. "She can wait until nine and go to the big store. I hate this town. In Los Angeles you can shop any time you like. But I suppose you're used to living like this."

"The grocery stores in Seattle are open all night, too," I said, falling neatly into the trap.

Aunt Norma smirked. "Well, that started in L.A.," she said.

I wanted to yell that not everything in the entire world started in L.A. Good taste, for one. But Mom had given me a significant look, so I said instead, "Mom, I'll finish packing the stuff in the linen closet first."

"And we'll try to finish up the rest of the house this afternoon," Mom said.

It was as if Aunt Norma wasn't there. Or was a piece of furniture. She contributed nothing to any conversation about work.

I could see where Ricki got her charm.

The real estate man came a few minutes early, unfortunately, and that made for instant bad feelings. Aunt Norma, still not dressed but wearing all her diamond rings, began a long monologue about real estate prices in dear old L.A., and what her friends thought she should do about selling her mother's house. No one paid any attention. The real estate man looked as if he'd heard it all before.

I was embarrassed and wished that just once Aunt Norma might guess that she was not as attractive and interesting as she thought she was.

"Have you got a list?" I whispered to Mom. "I'll go to the store now."

"Take your time," Mom said as she handed me the list and a handful of bills.

I'd left my denim jacket in the hall closet, so at least I didn't have to look at that lazy lump upstairs under the blankets again. I grabbed it and an umbrella and ran.

The white cat slunk away when I came out on the porch. Poor wet thing. I'd get cat food, too.

I didn't go straight to the grocery store, but walked around town instead. There weren't many tourists in sight, and the few I saw scurried along between shops, ducking the rain and looking disgusted. Between buildings, I could see the marina boats on the rough Sound.

"If I had known it would be this cold . . ." a woman was saying to a man as they passed me. They wore shorts, and their legs looked purplish and rough with goose bumps.

I hoped I'd see Carey, but I didn't. I didn't see anyone else I knew, either, until I turned a corner to one of the streets that led toward the water and the amusement park. Halfway down the block, outside a bakery, I caught a glimpse of Owen Norris, talking with the two tall boys Pete Striker had been arguing with at the park the other night.

Owen and the boys were laughing. Obviously, they were friends.

I hesitated, but Owen saw me and shouted my name. I smiled

and approached him reluctantly. One of the boys recognized me—
I could tell when his expression changed.

"Jane Douglas, meet a couple of friends of mine from Seattle,"
Owen said. "This is Kirk Jacobi and Sam Carpenter. They play basketball at my school."

The boy called Sam smiled. He still didn't recognize me. But
Kirk, the other boy, the one who had scuffled with Pete, only nodded. Owen noticed the chill, and for a moment his smile faded.

But then he seemed to brush away the feeling and grinned down
at me. "What are you doing here in the big city?"

"Grocery shopping," I said. "But I guess I passed the store without noticing."

"I bet you were really looking for me," he said.

Not you, oh not you, I thought, and I was miserable for him because
I knew that he liked me more than I liked him.

"Nope, I'm looking for a loaf of whole wheat bread," I said,
consulting my list. "And milk, orange juice, cereal, and cat food."

"We'll help," Owen offered.

But Kirk raised his hands in protest. "We've gotta go," he said.
"Catch up with you later, Owen." And before his friend could
agree or disagree, Kirk hurried toward the hotel closest to the marina.

"Wait a sec!" Sam yelled after him. "Sorry!" he apologized, but
he took off after his friend.

Owen looked puzzled, but he didn't say anything, and I was
grateful for that.

"Well, come on," he said. "Let's go shopping."

I laughed. "You don't need to help me. I think I can handle it myself."

"Hey, if my mother is skulking around anywhere and sees me honestly employed by someone, she'll be so impressed she'll let me out of leg irons at night. If we see her, give me a dime as fast as you can, and I'll show her that I'm not what she says I am."

"Which is?" I asked, just as he'd meant me to.

"Let's see if I get it straight," he said, pretending to think hard and recall the words exactly. "I'm the 'laziest human being ever to sit down in front of a television set and hook himself up to a ventilator so he doesn't even have to bother with breathing.'"

I burst out laughing. "I'll tell that to my mother," I said. "She likes a funny story."

"Oh, thank you, thank you," Owen said, bowing. "That's what I need, a girl who helps her mother understand and appreciate me."

We had a good time. We laughed all the way through the grocery store, until I'm sure the people working there were glad to see us leave. And we laughed all the way home, too.

But he wasn't Carey. I couldn't take Carey home with me.

I noticed that the car belonging to the real estate agent was gone. But Aunt Norma's new rental car was still there. Should I invite Owen in? Aunt Norma was so embarrassing. And I already knew from the way he ignored Ricki in the restaurant that he didn't like her.

"While I'm here, I'll tell your mother about tonight's specials at the restaurant," Owen offered as we went through the front door. "That way there'll be enough time for you guys to drive over to

Port Shasta. Just don't eat at the Captain's Grille, because my uncle owns that, too, and that's where he sends the leftovers."

Mom was taking down the china set that Aunt Norma wanted and packing it. I could hear Aunt Norma arguing with Ricki somewhere.

"Hi, Owen," Mom said when she saw him. "I hope you're staying for lunch. It's peanut butter sandwiches and canned peaches."

Owen pretended to stagger back a step, but he said, "I could use a gourmet meal like that, Mrs. Douglas. Thanks."

Ricki came in, dressed in gold tights and a black tunic. "Oh," she said, doing her best to sound startled. "I thought Carey was here."

Perhaps it was only my imagination, but it seemed to me as if the sentence hit the floor like a manhole cover.

I stared at Ricki and she smirked back.

"Who's Carey?" Mom asked at the same moment I began talking.

"Owen, let's go back downtown and have hamburgers. My treat. I owe you for carrying home the groceries. Come on. Let's go."

"How about me?" Ricki drawled.

I shot her a look that would have killed anybody else.

"See you in a little bit, Mom," I said. "I'll finish up the closet when I get back."

I shut the door and took a deep breath.

"I guess you talked your way out of that one," Owen said as he ran down the steps.

I gave him my most grateful look. "I guess I did."

Chapter Nine

"Who's this Carey?" Owen asked as soon as we were out of earshot.

My tongue seemed to stick to the roof of my mouth. "He's a boy Ricki and I met," I said vaguely. I had a strong hunch that Owen wouldn't think much of how and where I'd met Carey.

"I take it that your mom doesn't like him," Owen said. I wondered what he really thought.

"Mom doesn't know him," I said. I wanted to leave it at that.

"But Ricki is pretty sure your mom *won't* like him," Owen said. "So she thought she'd play that good old game, 'let's you and her fight.' Am I right?"

"You're exactly right," I said. "But do we have to talk about it?"

"Hey, I can live with that," he said. "People like your cousin make me nervous, and if I get nervous, I lose my appetite. Where should we eat?"

"You decide," I said. I'd already lost my appetite and couldn't stop thinking about what might happen when I got home. And what Ricki was saying behind my back.

We ate hamburgers in a small restaurant overlooking the amusement park. The park was closed, and it looked worse than ever in the rain, shabby and cheap and somehow dangerous.

"Do you like amusement parks?" Owen asked.

I shook my head. "Not really. When I was a kid, I liked going on the rides, but they're not much fun anymore, and the places always look so awful."

"I checked this one out a couple of years ago when I was here with my family. It's not much, except for the video games. My uncle says the owner's tearing it down next winter and enlarging the marina."

Where would the kids hang out then, I wondered.

"Did you meet this Carey in the amusement park?" Owen asked. He swallowed the last bite of his hamburger and waited for my answer, his gaze directed over my shoulder.

I was accustomed to being open with people, and my first impulse was to admit where I'd met Carey. But instead, I said, "Is this a final, or just a pop quiz?"

Owen laughed. "Don't you hate people who ask too many questions? Sorry. Do you want dessert? I'm still hungry."

"I can't eat another thing, but you go ahead and order. I'll watch you eat and make *you* nervous."

"You're a hard woman," he said. "You know how to break a guy down."

I didn't care how long he took to eat his dessert. I was in no hurry to find out what was happening back at the house, because I knew there was nothing I could do, one way or another, if Ricki had decided to entertain herself by ruining my life.

I convinced Owen that I didn't need any more help from him, so I walked home alone through another rainstorm, soaked to the skin. And expecting the worst.

As soon as I got through the front door, Mom said, "You forgot the umbrella, didn't you? Run up and change clothes."

I took a deep breath, relieved. Everything seemed to be all right—so far. "Did you settle everything with the real estate agent?" I called out as I ran upstairs.

"No," Mom said. She sounded older. And tired.

The house around me was silent. Ricki was in our room, applying makeup in front of the dresser mirror. She glanced at me with distaste when I closed the door behind me.

"Boy, are you wet," she said.

I began pulling off my clothes without answering her.

"Aren't you curious?" she asked.

"About what?"

She laughed. "About whether or not I told your mother about Carey."

"I know you didn't," I said as I pulled on a T-shirt and a cardigan. "She would have said something as soon as I came in."

"You sound sure of yourself," she said.

I zipped up my dry jeans. "Ricki, I don't want to play games with you. I just want to finish work on the house and get back to Seattle."

"But what about Carey?" she asked. "Don't you want to see him tonight?"

That was more important to me than anything else. But admitting it to her could only be a mistake.

"We'll see," I said. I caught myself touching my bare earlobe and stopped. But Ricki had seen the gesture, and she grinned knowingly.

Aunt Norma took Ricki out to lunch, but they came back an hour later, to our surprise. While we worked, Mom had speculated that we wouldn't see them for the rest of the day.

"I hate that car," Aunt Norma announced as soon as she returned. "We came back rather than take a chance driving to Port Shasta."

Mom sighed and stood up, wiping her dusty hands on the towel tied around her waist.

"Maybe you should stay here, Norma," she said. "Mrs. Soriano could come back this afternoon to set the time to pick everything up."

Aunt Norma stared. "I don't like her. I think we could do better selling the things ourselves."

Mom shook her head. "It's too late now. It's out of our hands."

"Well, you can't expect *me* to go along with something I don't understand," Aunt Norma said. "And I've stayed here too long already. I'm certain Ruby Bennet didn't waste a minute taking out after Milt when I left."

She was so upset that she didn't notice all the different emotions flickering over Mom's face.

"Then let's let Mrs. Soriano take the furniture and have it over with," Mom said. I thought she sounded a little too eager. Aunt Norma would pick up on it.

"I don't know," Aunt Norma said vaguely. "I didn't like that real estate agent, either. He's probably in on this with that man the judge turned everything over to. They're all in it together. My friends warned me."

"The 'For Sale' sign goes up tomorrow or the next day," Mom said.

"I don't know why you can't see reason," Aunt Norma said. "But then, what's new about that? Mother always said you couldn't see your big feet until you fell over them."

She grabbed Ricki's arm and rushed out, banging the door, without giving Mom a chance to answer. Hit and run.

"Never mind, Mom," I said.

"I knew she'd make this an uphill job, and we'd end up doing everything ourselves." She pressed her fingers against her mouth, and I wondered if she was ready to cry. The idea horrified me. I'd never seen my mother cry.

"We're doing all the work and Aunt Norma is doing all the deciding," I said, to fill the silence.

"She doesn't decide *anything*," Mom protested.

"She does it by *not* deciding anything," I said. Suddenly I was angry with Mom. "What's wrong with you?" I demanded. "Can't you see that's how she controls you? She lets things hang, just like Miss O'Brien in fourth grade. She always made me wait and wait before she'd sign my pass so I could go to the symphony's open rehearsal with the rest of the kids in the orchestra. She didn't care how upset I got when I never knew if I could go until the last minute. Or maybe she did know, and she liked hurting me that much. Can't you see that Aunt Norma is doing the same thing to you?"

Mom wrote something on a box with a black pen. "Norma learned that from our mother," she said. "I was the one who got stuck taking care of everything, and they hung back, begging for help and then criticizing the results, and I had to start all over again."

"Was that why you didn't see much of her?" I asked.

"When I left for college, I promised myself I'd stay away, and I did," she said. "Sometimes I was sorry that you didn't get to know my mother very well. You should have known both your grandmothers. But your other grandmother is so different, so easy to be around. She's not manipulative, not . . ."

I waited while Mom sorted out her thoughts.

She gave up and shook her head. "I felt guilty when Mother died. Your dad and I had only been here twice after we got married—and even then, we invited ourselves. She made us feel like intruders. Which is what we were, I guess. What a stupid waste."

"Are you sure it doesn't bother you, going through her things?" I asked.

"No, it doesn't," Mom said. "Maybe having Norma drag this mess out for two years was good. It gave me time to get over feeling guilty and regretting a lot of things. Now if we can just finish everything and put an end to it, I'll feel as if I'm escaping from something."

You will be, I thought. And I'll be escaping from Ricki. But what about Carey?

"Women should stick up for each other," Mom said, almost to herself. "Especially sisters. I can't understand why they don't. The world is such a hard place—life is so hard. Men stick together and defend each other, but women don't. It's as if we're still living in some other age, when we needed to compete and manipulate in order to survive. Jane—listen to me. Don't let what you are be decided by anyone else. Be independent. Always." But her fingers massaged her forehead. Her face was pale.

Oh, Mom, I thought. Why can't you be independent then, and throw Aunt Norma out? Why are you so careful around her?

We had started cleaning the two unused bedrooms when Aunt Norma and Ricki came back. I was vacuuming the carpet in the small bedroom next to the one Mom shared with Aunt Norma when Ricki popped through the door, yelled my name, and reached around me to turn off the vacuum cleaner.

She startled me. I'd been thinking about Carey again, wondering if his eyes were the exact color of my mother's moonstone, or if that was only a fantasy of mine.

"Come on," Ricki said. "Norma wants to have dinner early and rent a couple of videos. She can't stand this weather."

I was hungry, but I needed a shower before I could go anywhere. "Did she talk to Mom?" I asked.

"They're having a big argument right now," Ricki said, laughing. "It never stops, does it?"

"It could," I said. "It sure could."

"But what would be the fun in that?" Ricki asked.

I shook my head, disgusted. I didn't understand people who loved uproars.

"If it's still raining tonight, do you want to go to the amusement park?" she asked.

"Shh," I hissed. "Are you crazy? They might hear you."

"Well, do you? I saw Dennis when Norma and I were coming out of that tacky little gift shop across from the marina. He was across the street and I don't think he saw me. Norma would have had a fit if he'd come over to talk."

She seemed so pleased and excited at the prospect of her mother having a fit that I seriously wondered what was wrong with her.

"I don't think he's the sort of boy she'd want you mixed up with," I said.

"And Carey *is?*" she asked.

"He's different and you know it," I said.

"Is he?" she asked. "Are you so sure?"

I couldn't answer. I reached out to turn the vacuum cleaner on again, but she put her hand over mine.

"You're not still mad, are you?" she asked softly. "Don't be. Sometimes I get upset and say things I'm sorry for afterward. We're a lot alike, you know. Our mothers' feud has rubbed off on us, but we don't need to fight. We've got something in common. We've got the park."

I turned on the vacuum cleaner to make a wall of noise between us. Part of me was relieved by what she said. And the other part of me wondered where my common sense had gone. She was trying to manipulate me again.

I didn't like my cousin. But I needed her if I was going to continue seeing Carey at night. If she grew angry enough to actually tell Mom . . .

How did I get myself into this?

When I finished vacuuming, I opened a can of cat food, dumped it on a saucer with a chipped gold edge, and carried it out to the back porch. The bowl was empty. I replaced it with the saucer, called out, "Here, kitty, kitty," and waited. The cat didn't come. Disappointed, I went back inside.

We had an early dinner in the Chinese restaurant and stopped by the video store on the way home. Aunt Norma picked out two videos, but Mom paid the rental. She also paid for the popcorn Aunt Norma and Ricki wanted. Why was I not surprised?

It occurred to me as we were riding home that Mom had run away once, but she couldn't *get* away.

Aunt Norma settled down in front of the TV with her popcorn. Mom, looking so tired that she almost seemed ill, watched the movie for a while and then said she couldn't stay awake any longer. Even though it was still light outside, she went to bed.

Aunt Norma turned the sound up louder and smiled to herself.

Ricki and I shared a small bowl of popcorn, side by side on the sofa. She nudged me and I nudged her back. We exchanged small smiles. I hated myself for befriending the enemy, but Carey was somewhere, waiting for dark, and so was I.

Oh, rain stop and twilight fall, I thought. I want to see the lights in the park and hear the carousel music. I want to reach out and take Carey's hand tonight. Because if not tonight, then when?

We might go back to Seattle as soon as the day after tomorrow. Unless Aunt Norma refused to make up her mind.

Chapter Ten

The rain stopped, but the sky remained overcast, and twilight seemed to fall earlier than it had the night before. Aunt Norma lost interest in the second video and turned it off.

"Norma," Ricki whined, "we were watching that."

"I'm exhausted and going up to bed," Aunt Norma said. "I wouldn't be able to sleep if you two were down here, making a lot of racket."

Ricki jumped up, "Oh, all right. Have it your way. You always do."

She ran up the stairs ahead of her mother. I stayed behind, rewound the tape and removed it from the VCR, and turned out the downstairs lights. My heart beat quickly and too hard.

Soon.

Ricki changed clothes twice before we left, each time posing and studying her reflection in the mirror.

"I'm running out of clothes," she said.

I didn't say anything, and wouldn't let myself look around the room at all the discarded garments. Instead, I picked up my book and read.

After a while, Aunt Norma stopped going back and forth between bedroom and bath, and she seemed to be in bed at last.

Ricki was impatient. "Come on, let's go."

"Give them a chance to fall asleep this time," I said. It was still early, barely after nine. I, too, was eager to leave, but I didn't want to take risks now, not with time running out so quickly.

Through the window, I saw the amusement park lights and the Ferris wheel turning, turning, drizzling enchantment into the night. This was fairyland again, not the shabby, vulgar place I had seen when I was eating lunch with Owen.

What is the truth about it? I wondered. Is it what I saw in daylight, with safe, laughing Owen across from me? Or what I see at night while I'm waiting to join the silver-eyed boy?

I put on my earrings and didn't care that Ricki saw me do it.

Carey was waiting for us inside the amusement park gate. No, Carey was waiting for *me*. Ricki didn't bother saying anything more than a quick "hi" to him before she hurried away, waving to Dennis and Pete who were hanging out in front of the video arcade, smoking and snickering together over something.

"You look so nice," Carey said quietly. "I like watching you walk toward me. When it was raining today, I wondered if you'd want to come tonight. I was afraid you wouldn't."

"The rain has stopped," I said, looking up at him.

"Has it?" he said, laughing. "I don't see anything but you."

It was the most romantic thing anyone had ever said to me, and in that moment, I was afraid, so afraid, that I'd never hear anything like it again, not from anyone, not even from him. The moment, which should have been filled with joy, was filled instead with a terrible sadness. This wouldn't, couldn't, be the last time I'd see him. But before a week was over, he would be part of my past.

We walked through the park and back again, stopping for a few minutes to talk to Meg and Ellie. Or rather, we talked and they looked away, as if they were preoccupied, or angry with us.

"Have you seen my brother?" Ellie demanded of Carey. "He disappeared after we got here."

"We saw him with Dennis," Carey said.

"He said he'd give back the money he borrowed," Ellie complained. She didn't look at Carey. "He promised he'd pay up tonight."

Meg's gaze slid toward me but she didn't speak. She seemed tense, as if waiting for something to happen. There were always uncomfortable undercurrents when I was around the amusement park kids. But I wasn't curious about them. I didn't want to know them any better or become involved in their problems.

Carey shrugged and told Ellie that Pete and Dennis were back near the gate.

"Near the arcade," Ellie scoffed. She yanked irritably at her short jacket, brushed off a coarse thread, and yanked at it again. "Come on, Meg, before Pete and Dennis spend everything they've got."

They hurried away and I felt sorry for them instead of being annoyed at how they ignored me so pointedly. They were like grimy versions of Ricki, gaudy and full of secrets I didn't want to explore.

Left alone again, Carey and I walked close to the water. I wondered if he'd take my hand. Or put his arm around me. Instead, he bent to snatch up a few pebbles, and then, one by one, he tossed them across the beach.

"How are you and your mother coming along with getting the house ready to sell?" he asked.

"We've gone through all the closets and the attic," I said. "Now we have to finish cleaning."

"So you could be going home any time," he said.

"Yes," I said. "But not tomorrow." Aunt Norma had guaranteed that by her behavior.

A chill washed over me and I hugged myself.

"I'll be leaving the first of July," he said.

I remembered that he wanted to spend the summer with his father in Montana.

"But you'll be coming back here before school starts," I said. It wouldn't matter because I would be somewhere else, seeing different streets and another part of the Sound. He'd be out of my life.

"No, I won't come back to Royal Bay this time," he said. "Dad's moving to Connecticut, and I'm going with him."

Connecticut! But that was on the other side of the country!

I swallowed hard. My ears were ringing.

He moved a step closer, so that his arm touched mine. "My dad called this afternoon and asked if I wanted to go with him when he moves. I could go to a better school, maybe even start college early. My mother thinks it's a good idea, too."

He didn't belong here, in this old cannery town turned tourist trap. He belonged where the schools were wonderful, where he'd find other kids like himself, interesting people who read as much as he did and wanted all the things that cities have to offer. He needed to escape from Royal Bay, the way my mother had.

She might like him after all. If there was only some way of getting around explaining that he had picked me up in the amusement park she hated so much.

But I was leaving, and then he'd be leaving, and there was no point in introducing him to my mother. No point in telling my secret and risking so much.

"I guess you'll miss your friends," I said, and hated myself for hinting around to learn if he'd miss me.

"Sure, I guess," he said. He didn't sound convinced himself.

We wandered back toward the Ferris wheel, both of us silent and ill-at-ease now. Reality does that to people. Clocks and calendars. No matter how dark the night and how loud the music, the clock keeps ticking.

My cousin was in line at the ticket counter, along with Meg and Ellie, Pete and Dennis. They yelled to us, and we joined them. The park wasn't crowded, but it seemed as if half the people there had decided to buy tickets at the same time. I studied the tourists, trying to pretend they interested me, trying not to think beyond that moment.

"Hey, Ricki, didn't you say the Ferris wheel was boring?" Dennis asked. He grinned at her, challenging her.

"There are rides that are more exciting," she said. "*Lots* of things are more exciting."

Dennis laughed a little and moved closer to her. Apparently he was interested in her again. Or perhaps he was one of those boys who thought girls were interchangeable—and disposable. "Tell me what you think is more exciting," he said.

"You mean *here,* at the amusement park?" Ricki asked. Her smile glittered. Her eyes were bright with anticipation.

"Anywhere," Dennis said, dropping one shoulder, inviting her to move closer, too. "Tell me what you think is exciting."

Meg and Ellie drew together, as if for protection. I suspected that Ricki was better at flirting than anyone they'd ever seen. She certainly beat anyone I'd seen.

Carey shook his head, then looked away.

"Hey, hey," Pete said suddenly. He sounded angry. He was looking toward a group of young people straggling down the center of the park.

It was Owen! And the two tall boys he'd introduced me to when we went shopping, the boys Pete had disliked so much.

I hoped Owen didn't see me, but he had. He raised his hand in greeting.

"You know him?" Pete demanded of me, angry before he'd even heard my answer.

"Sure," I said. I didn't like his tone of voice or his attitude. But I didn't want trouble either. "He works in the restaurant where my mother and I eat sometimes."

"He's got an attitude," Ricki told Pete eagerly. "He's got a yard and a half of attitude, and I don't like him."

I stared at her. Was she trying to start something? She must have known that Pete was temperamental.

"He hangs out with Kirk Jacobi?" Pete demanded.

I had to explain before Pete transferred his anger from Kirk to Owen. "They go to the same school in Seattle," I babbled. "Kirk and Sam are here with their parents, and Owen ran into them."

Now Dennis was interested. He looked at me strangely and said, "Sounds like you've been going around with the wrong people."

Ricki's eyes were hard and bright, and she didn't blink. I felt trapped, not sure where to try and take the conversation. I wasn't good at this sort of thing.

Owen was close enough to talk to us now. "Hey, Jane, Ricki," he said. "You having a good time?"

Oh, poor Owen, I thought, despairing already. Couldn't he sense what was going on right here and now? His friends, wiser than he, dropped back a full step and didn't smile or greet anyone.

Pete's tan eyes were narrowed, his jaw set. Dennis rocked back and forth, and he seemed eager, almost electric. They enjoyed the tension. They wanted to be angry at someone about something, because of what might come afterward.

Like Ricki. She, too, was excited. She licked her lips and smiled, showing those small, sharp teeth.

"Owen, this is my friend, Carey," I said quickly, before I lost my courage. "We're going on the Ferris wheel."

"We came for the video games," Owen said. Now I could see that he had picked up the bad feelings. His voice sounded nervous. "See you guys later."

Carey nodded and smiled. "See you later, Owen."

"Do you know those boys, Jane?" Ricki asked. She wasn't going to let this die. Her little pink tongue flicked out, tasting trouble and liking it.

I shook my head, unable to speak.

Pete glared after Owen and his friends. "They think they're . . ."

"Are you going on the Ferris wheel, Pete?" his sister asked loudly. She nudged him. "The seats hold two people. How are we going to sit? There are seven of us, so one of us will have to sit alone."

Ricki was distracted now. "I can't sit alone," she said. "I hate being stuck up on top when they stop it to let other people on. I *won't* ride alone."

"Who said you had to be alone?" Dennis asked as he slipped his arm around her waist, but he was watching Owen and his friends disappear into the crowd.

"*I'm* not sitting alone, either," Ellie cried.

"Neither am I," Meg said.

It was clear that someone would have to sit alone or not take the ride. I wanted to spend that time with Carey, but by the time the discussion ended, Carey had volunteered to stay behind and no one argued. The only reward I got for this loss was the quick squeeze he gave my hand as the ticket-taker unfastened the chain at the small gate and let me through—with Ricki. In spite of the way Carey's presence always distracted me, I had still seen Ricki maneuver Dennis into a seat with Ellie.

Ellie and Dennis were already high above us. Meg and Pete waited behind.

A young man who smelled of garlic helped us into a seat and fastened the safety bar. He smiled at Ricki. She ignored him.

When the wheel began moving, Ricki said, "I bet you had a big romantic moment all planned."

"No, of course not," I lied. I fingered the earrings nervously.

Ricki laughed. "Well, he's cute, all right. Carey, I mean. But he's too quiet. Now Dennis, he's the exciting one. And he's bad. Maybe even dangerous. A girl could have a lot of fun with somebody like him."

"Your mother would have a fit if she heard you saying that," I said.

Ricki smirked. "Norma? Well, sure, she'd be mad because he's a small-town kid with no future. But she can't complain about me. She's been married so many times she can't keep all her names straight. And this new guy of hers—he's way too young for her, for one thing. If he's still interested in her when we get home, I'm going to tell her that he makes me nervous, watching me when I'm alone in the pool."

I gawked at her. "Is that true?"

She giggled. "No, but she'll go crazy trying to figure out what to do about it. He's rich. She won't want to give that up."

"Maybe you shouldn't interfere," I said, as if it was any of my business.

"Oh, come on, haven't you ever had any fun driving your mother crazy?" she demanded.

"No," I said. "I hate fighting. I get a stomachache and feel miserable."

"You're missing a lot," Ricki said. "Try it some time. Why don't you let it slip that you've been sneaking out, and see what she does?"

"I already know what she'd do," I blurted. "She'd be furious with me and she wouldn't let me come back."

The moment I said it, I was sorry. It wasn't as if Ricki didn't already suspect that Mom would react that way. But putting something into words can be risky. Words make it real. Then your enemies have a weapon to use against you.

"Maybe I'll tell her," Ricki said slowly, savoring her words. "What fireworks! Your mom would be mad at both of us and Norma would defend me—she always does—and then we could put an end to this rotten vacation and go home."

"Your mother was supposed to help . . ." I began angrily. "She has to stay."

"She doesn't *have* to do anything." Ricki said. "She told me that before we left. She isn't going to let your mother bully her into selling things for half of what they're worth, just because your mother wants the money so much. It's not our fault that your family needs it."

My face flamed. "Not as much as your mother does. For the last two years she's been complaining to my mother that she needs the money . . ."

"Oh, shut up, shut up!" Ricki cried. "Do you know how tired I am of you and your smug expression and your snotty mother and . . . and your stupid moonstone earrings!"

Before I could stop her, she grabbed the one Carey had given me, pulled the loop out of my earlobe, and, while I tried to snatch it back, threw it off the Ferris wheel.

"You're crazy!" I yelled. "You are really crazy! Why did you do that?"

"You think I don't know about the great earring tragedy? Oh, big deal, Jane. Big deal. Just think about this as a family tradition. When I tell Norma about it, she'll die laughing over me getting even for her all over again."

I'd never been so angry before, or so close to slapping someone. What had I ever done to her to make her want to treat me that way?

Other than being my mother's daughter.

I wanted the Ferris wheel to stop as soon as we got to the bottom so I could look for the earring, somewhere out there in the crowd. It stopped, but not because the man had seen my earring disappear. He threw us off for yelling at each other and causing a disturbance.

"Don't come back," he said, glaring at us. "I don't want to see the two of you around here again, understand?"

"As if we cared," Ricki retorted.

I looked around for Carey, embarrassed and wondering if he'd seen anything, but I couldn't find him. Ricki clopped away in her ridiculous high heels, and I started toward the place where I thought my earring might have fallen.

A dozen people stood there in a little knot. They seemed to know each other—and they stared at me with open curiosity. Humiliated, I kept my eyes on the ground, but I didn't see my earring anywhere.

Ricki had to be cut out of everything, because she wanted to ruin things. I would have to find a way to meet Carey on my own as many times as I could before Mom and I left.

And I'd have to tell him about the earring.

"Hey," he said, startling me.

"I was looking for you," I said.

"On the ground?" he asked, laughing.

How could I tell him what a jerk my cousin was? But how long would it be before he noticed that my earring was missing?

I took a deep breath. "I'm looking for the earring you gave me," I said.

"Did you drop it?" he asked.

I told him the truth.

We searched for a long time, but didn't find the earring. "We need to look in daylight," he said. "I'll come back tomorrow. I know you can't, but maybe I'll find it. And maybe somebody will turn it in to the lost and found."

"I feel terrible," I said. "I loved that earring."

"Moonstones," he said, and he smiled down at me suddenly,

devastating me completely. He touched my mother's earring. "I'll always think of you when I see one."

His hand slid over my shoulder, down my arm, and closed around my hand. "Let's have hot chocolate, and then I'll walk you all the way home this time."

"Ricki is around somewhere, laughing at me," I said bitterly.

"No, she took off," he said. "I saw her leave the park. I'm glad she's gone, because now we can have time alone, without expecting her to interrupt us any minute."

I smiled at him, and I reminded myself that I should be grateful for this brief evening, and for the few hours we had left. I wasn't sure how I'd feel when it was over, but we had at least one more night, and maybe time enough so that we could tell each other all the things we needed to say.

Over our hot chocolate, I told him that I planned to take *Ishmael* home. "I know I'll want to read it again," I said.

"You could wait for the movie," he said.

Both of us laughed. For a while, I forgot how awful the park was, and how uneasy I felt about the other people there. Carey and I sat in a bright circle of light, watching each other's faces, and nothing else mattered.

Chapter Eleven

I stayed at the park with Carey for a dangerous hour. I was risking anything and everything that Ricki might think of saying back at the house. But finally I couldn't push my worry away any longer, and I told Carey I had to go home.

We walked along the beach in silence, holding hands as if we were afraid to let go. Ahead, in my grandmother's house, I could see a light on upstairs in my bedroom. I didn't know what it meant, but I was sick with worry.

Halfway up the hill, Carey stopped me.

"Look," he said. "Promise me that you'll tell me before you leave town. Promise that you won't just go and leave me wondering what happened."

"We didn't have the phone connected, remember? How can I get in touch with you?"

"I'll be helping my mother in the shop until I leave," he said. "You could stop by. Even if I'm not there, you could tell her that you're going."

"She knows about me?" I asked, startled.

"Sure. I had to say something about staying out this late. She hates it when I come here, but she liked what I said about you."

I was embarrassed. He had told his mother about me, but I'd kept him a secret, as if I was ashamed of him.

"Before I go, you can come by the house and meet Mom," I said. "Maybe tomorrow."

He shook his head. "No, I have a hunch how much trouble it could cause. It doesn't sound good, our hanging out here."

"I'll tell her I met you in town."

"And you think your cousin will let you get away with it?"

I glanced up at the house—and my lighted window. I'd be lucky if she hadn't already told Mom.

"I'll stop by the shop," I told him. "If you're not there, I'll leave a message with your mother. And my address in Seattle, too. Maybe you could write to me and let me know where you'll be."

He put both arms around me and pulled me against his chest and rested his chin on my hair.

I slid my arms around his waist and hid my smile against his jacket. No matter what, I'd always have this moment to remember.

"Jane," he whispered.

I looked up, straight into his eyes. For a long time, we studied each others' faces, memorizing what we saw. Then he smiled suddenly, bent his head and kissed me.

"Jane," he whispered again, this time against my lips. "Remember me."

———

"I'll see you tomorrow night," I said.

"Are you sure?"

"We aren't ready to leave yet," I said. "I'm sure I can be there."

"And if your mother knows about us?"

The fear of it took my breath away. "I'll find some way to explain that I have to see you again," I said. Dimly, I wondered if Mom had felt this way once. If it had even been possible for anyone to have felt this way.

He watched while I hurried back to the house, slipped in the door and up the stairs, almost too afraid to breathe. I could hear Ricki's little radio playing in our room, and the thudding of my heart nearly drowned it out.

Where was my mother? The hall was dark, and as far as I could tell, her door was shut.

I opened mine.

"Well, well, home at last," Ricki said without bothering to lower her voice. She sat on her bed in her bra and panties, painting her toenails. She'd spilled nail polish on the spread.

Anger engulfed me again, and I couldn't speak. I couldn't have said a word if my life depended on it. I simply changed into my pajamas and got into bed.

"Not washing up tonight?" she asked. "Not brushing your hair a hundred strokes like Mommy taught you?"

I turned my back and pulled my sheet over my head.

She was crazy, she and her mother both.

After a long time, she turned off her radio and put out the lights.

"Nighty-night," she said, laughing. "Bet I sleep better than you do. *You've* got to stay awake wondering if I told your mother."

Mom would have stayed up if Ricki had told, I thought. Wouldn't she?

Wouldn't she?

Ricki was right. I stayed awake.

I got up at seven, before anyone else, and showered quickly. Ricki was a lump under her covers again, and I couldn't guess if she was awake or not.

After I dressed, I hurried down to the kitchen and carried the cat food can out to the deck. The saucer was empty, as I had hoped, and I filled it again, but I didn't see the cat.

Before I was halfway through my cereal, Mom came in, yawning and finger-combing her hair.

"I don't know how you can sleep, with that radio of Ricki's playing half the night," she said. "Norma says it helps Ricki sleep in spite of the pain in her back, but I bet it keeps the rest of the town awake."

"She's pathetic," I said. "The reason she can't sleep is because she naps so much during the day. But pretty soon we'll be on our way home and I'll do my best to forget I know her."

"You sound a little bitter," Mom said. She put a cup of water in the microwave. "What's going on?"

She didn't know! Carey was still my secret.

"It's not worth talking about," I said. "What's going on here today?"

Mom got the instant coffee out of the refrigerator. "Mrs. Soriano will come today for sure, and we'll set the time for picking up the furniture."

"If Aunt Norma lets you," I said. I was exhausted, and couldn't keep the anger out of my voice. "She's been acting like a jerk for two years. Why should she stop now?"

"Because she says she really needs money," Mom said. "I don't know what her other problems are. Maybe they have something to do with this being the last chance she'll ever have to control me. Maybe she can't give it up."

"Dad told you that before we left," I said. I took a deep breath. "Maybe you could call him and ask him to come. He'll straighten Aunt Norma out and decide things."

Mom fixed her coffee and tasted it before she answered. "You know that if he takes his leave time now, we'll miss our trip."

"Maybe it would be worth it," I said, thinking only of having more time with Carey.

Mom raised her eyebrows. "I thought you were crazy about going to Canada."

"I am," I said. "But I hate what's going on here. Aunt Norma might even get mad enough to leave if Dad shows up. You know how much she hates him."

"I can't count on that solving anything. Norma manages to complicate just about everything."

Aunt Norma came in then, flustered. "What about me? What do I complicate?"

Mom's gaze slid guiltily toward me, then back to her sister. "Today's the day we decide when the furniture will be picked up, Norma," she said briskly. "Jane and I have to get back to Seattle, and I've been thinking . . ."

"My friends told me to hold out for the best prices," Aunt Norma said.

"Norma, this isn't your friends' furniture, it's ours. It's in a different state. Things aren't the same here. Your friends' experiences don't count." Mom sounded as if she was ready to cry.

"That's what *you* say," Aunt Norma said petulantly. "I don't feel right about giving away my mother's possessions. And I still don't have the missing pieces of the china. Now you've got everything packed up in boxes, and I'll have to go through every one of them before I leave."

"I can't tell whether you want to leave or you want to stay," Mom cried, exasperated. "Which is it? One minute you're threatening to leave immediately, and the next moment, you want to unpack the boxes."

"Well, how do I know if you've packed up the china I want?" Aunt Norma asked. She looked around, scowling. "Didn't you make coffee? Why must we always have instant coffee?"

"Because I packed the coffee maker for Mrs. Soriano," Mom said. "And by the way, the box with your china has your name on it." She left the room carrying her cup.

I trailed after her. "Mom?"

"I'll definitely tell Mrs. Soriano to have the furniture picked up," she said. "And I'll go by the real estate agent's office and tell him to put up the sign."

"You can't do one thing unless I agree!" Aunt Norma cried from the kitchen.

As Mom started up the stairs, I saw tears spurt suddenly from her eyes.

I whirled around and caught Aunt Norma watching smugly from the kitchen doorway.

Her expression changed when she saw me watching. "Well, she can't," she said weakly. "I may leave details like this to other people, but still, I have to agree with what they do."

"What a fun game that must be," I said.

"What?" she asked. "What?"

I shook my head and followed Mom upstairs, but she had gone into the bathroom.

Ricki was still in bed when Mom and I left to return the videos and use a phone. Mom called Dad at his office and explained the situation, then listened while he talked.

"Okay," she said. "All right. I'll go ahead then, and we'll take it right up to the wire and see what she does. Do you want to talk to Jane?"

She handed me the phone. "Dad? How are you?"

"Missing my ladies," he said. "Henry isn't exactly great company. We don't agree on what we want to watch on TV. How's your mother holding up?"

I glanced over my shoulder and saw Mom watching me, as if she knew what he'd ask. "She's fine," I said. "She's determined."

"And how are you? Getting along with Ricki?"

I could taste gall. "I can't stand her," I said. "But it won't be forever."

He was quiet for a moment, and then he asked, "Do you and your mother need me there?"

I wanted to shout, "Yes!" We did need him, to shut up Aunt Norma and decide things—and maybe even delay things so that I could see Carey a few more times.

But I thought of Canada, and how much he wanted to go, and how hard he worked. "No, Dad," I said. "Mom's handling it."

"Norma gets to her," he said musingly.

"Mom's sassing back," I lied.

But Dad believed me. "Okay, Jane. I like the sound of that. But I'd really hoped everything would be settled by now."

"Soon," I said.

"Then you two should be home maybe the day after tomorrow," Dad said.

"You bet," I said, pretending I was enthusiastic.

After I told him good-bye, I looked back and saw Mom biting her lip.

"Mom, you okay?" I asked.

"I wish we were in Seattle," she said.

"Soon," I said again.

"I hate this town," she said. "I always did."

We ran into Mrs. Soriano outside the coffee shop. I waited while
Mom asked her when she would have the household furnishings
picked up.

A problem had developed. Someone named Frank, who was
supposed to be driving the furniture truck, was busy that afternoon
and the next morning.

"It'll have to be the day after, I'm afraid," Mrs. Soriano said re-
gretfully. "I hope it isn't too much of a hardship. I'll still leave your
beds and a few chairs. You said your next-door neighbor would let
me back in after you go so I can clear out the last of it?"

"Mrs. Phare has a key," Mom said. She was visibly disappointed.
"But I hate having the 'For Sale' sign put up while the house is full
of packing boxes."

We stopped at the real estate agent's office next, but he was out.
Mom left a message, asking him to come by the house, and then we
walked out into the sunlight.

In the hour since we'd left home, the town had filled up with
people dawdling through the small shops. I saw Kirk Jacobi across
the street, walking with an older man. If he saw me, he ignored me.

Mom and I bought sandwiches and a salad to bring home for
lunch. Most of the time Mom was silent. The line on her forehead
was deeper.

"It must have been hard for you, having Norma for a sister when
you were growing up," I said as we walked along Front Street.
"You never talked about what things were like when you were a
teenager."

"Growing up without a father was hard." We crossed an intersection and she looked out at the Sound. "I had this fantasy that if he hadn't died, he would have intervened."

"Intervened in what?" I asked.

Mom laughed, but her laugh sounded shaky. "That's just it," she said. "There wasn't anything to intervene in. There wasn't anything but years of silence from Mother and years of childish pettiness from Norma. It's not as if I needed a knight to protect me. I don't know what I needed."

"Escape," I said.

"Yes," she said, but she didn't smile, and I knew why. Aunt Norma still had power over her.

We ate alone because Aunt Norma had gone somewhere in her hated rental car and Ricki, sunning herself on the back porch, announced that she wouldn't eat small-town deli food if it was the last thing on earth to keep her from starvation.

As a reward for her attitude, Mom slammed the back door while my cousin was still talking. I had never seen her so angry.

Aunt Norma still hadn't returned by dinnertime, so Mom, Ricki, and I went into town without her. Mom insisted that we eat in our favorite restaurant in spite of Ricki's whining, and I smiled my brightest at Owen's nice mother as she led us to our table.

"The pepper steak is wonderful," she said. "And we've got pork roast, too."

"I'm starved," Mom said.

"I want a hamburger," Ricki said crossly. The restaurant didn't serve hamburgers.

"I . . ." I began.

Owen came up to clear the table next to us. Strangely, he didn't say hello, and he kept his back to us.

"Hey, Owen, what's new?" I called out to him.

He turned.

His face was bruised, one eye black, and his lower lip cut.

"What happened?" I cried.

He tried to smile, winced, and shook his head. "I didn't see the truck coming," he said, and then, without another word, he carried the tray away.

"He was beaten up by one of the town thugs," Mrs. Norris said angrily. "I wanted to call the police, but Owen wouldn't hear of it. He said it was something personal and he didn't want to discuss it with anybody, and nothing I say seems to change his mind."

I couldn't think straight. Fright rang in my ears like discordant bells. It was something personal? Who had done this to him?

Could it involve the amusement park kids?

I jumped up and followed Owen into the kitchen. He didn't see me at first, but a heavyset man in a white hat did, and he opened his mouth to shout at me.

"I have to see Owen!" I said.

Owen turned, astonished. "Jane? What do you want?"

"Who hit you?" I demanded. "Who was it? Why?"

He felt his lip gingerly. "It was a big yellow moving van . . ." he began.

"Was it one of the boys from the amusement park?" I asked.

He shook his head, then shrugged. "Pete Striker. You know. Big guy who hates other big guys? It's a basketball thing."

"You got into an argument with Pete over basketball?" I asked incredulously.

"Yeah, well, that and other things."

"Me?"

"You? No! Why?" He was genuinely astonished.

The man in the white hat was advancing on me. "You'll have to leave the kitchen, missy," he said.

"This isn't a missy," Owen told him. "It's that girl I was telling you about, the one I'm running away with as soon as you finally pay me all the money you owe me."

The man grinned at Owen reluctantly. "Fine, fine, go, go, run away if you want. But first, she has to get out of the kitchen."

"See you later, maybe," Owen said as I left.

When I got back to the table, Ricki was smirking. Mom looked concerned.

"How is he?" she asked.

"Fine, I guess," I said. "He said maybe he'd see me later."

"But what happened to him?" Mom asked.

"A boy beat him up," I said. "He wouldn't tell me why."

"Maybe he deserved it," Ricki said. "Maybe he's not as nice as he looks and hangs around the wrong sort of people."

"Oh, Ricki, for once shut up," Mom snapped.

Ricki's face turned red, and I didn't bother hiding my smile. If I'd been half as smart as I thought I was, I'd have known that Ricki would make sure I'd pay for that.

Owen didn't come out into the restaurant again.

Chapter Twelve

Aunt Norma still wasn't home when we got there. Mom asked Ricki if she had any idea when her mother would return, but Ricki only shrugged.

"Does she do this all the time?" I asked.

"Wow, are *you* crabby," Ricki said. "I wonder why. If I had boys fighting over me, I'd be wearing my best smile."

"Owen wasn't fighting over me," I cried.

"Jane?" Mom asked, her eyebrows lifted. "What did Owen tell you?"

I shot Ricki a look, but her malicious little smile told me that she had me right where she wanted me.

"I told you—he said a boy hit him, but I didn't get a chance to find out why, because his uncle told me to get out of the kitchen," I said.

"Some things don't change," Mom said. "This town always did have a lot of cheap thugs hanging around."

"You should know," Ricki singsonged, and before Mom could respond, she ran upstairs.

"What was that supposed to mean?" I asked. Mom turned to me, all the color drained from her face. "Mom, what *is* it?"

She touched her temples. "I need to get my pills. I thought I had them in my purse, but I couldn't find them when we were at the restaurant."

"I'll help you look," I said. "Could they be in your bedroom?"

"They must be," she said.

"Sit down in the kitchen and rest," I said, and I ran upstairs without waiting for her answer.

Ricki was waiting at the head of the stairs.

"Eavesdropping?" I asked as I brushed past her.

"Does your mommy have a headache again?" Ricki asked as she followed me down the short hall to the bedroom our mothers had been using.

I didn't answer, but opened the door and went straight to the dresser. Like the one in my room, it was littered with cosmetics, jewelry, and junk. None of it belonged to Mom.

"You and your mother are pigs," I said as I sorted through it.

No answer. I glanced over my shoulder and saw that I was alone in the room.

I finally located Mom's prescription bottle, in the pocket of her bathrobe. It was nearly empty.

Downstairs, I found her sitting at the kitchen table, sipping tea. I handed her the bottle and told her where I'd found it.

"I must be losing my mind," she said. She shook one of the pills into her palm. "I completely forgot where I'd left them."

I watched while she washed the pill down with a swallow of tea. "How long will it take to work?" I asked.

"Half an hour or more," she said. "If it works."

"You'd better go to bed," I said. "If you want to talk to Aunt Norma, write a note and leave it for her."

Mom managed a smile. "I can't imagine her bothering to read a note, any more than I can imagine her listening to her answering machine, or responding to a letter from a lawyer, or doing anything else that's responsible."

I sat down across from her. "I know," I said. "She leaves all that to other people."

Both of us managed to laugh.

"I always hoped Mother and Norma would change," Mom said. She looked into her cup as if she could find a solution to her problems there. "I always thought that if I helped them just once more, then the next time something went wrong, they'd know how to be independent and handle things themselves." She sipped her tea slowly.

"But how did your mother manage after you ran . . . after you left home?" I asked.

"I suppose she relied on the Phares and other people. There was always somebody who'd help her. And there's always been somebody who'd help Norma."

"Husbands," I said. "Lots and lots of husbands."

Mom laughed, then winced. "You'll have to stop being funny, at least until this headache goes away."

"Okay, I'll stop. But you've got to go to bed now. We can leave a light on for Aunt Norma."

"Heavens, yes," Mom said. "If we don't, she'll stand on the porch and shout until someone comes down and turns the lights on for her."

We left the porch and living room lights on, then climbed the stairs together.

"Get a good night's sleep," I told her.

"You, too," she said. She glanced down the hall toward my bedroom and grimaced. Ricki's radio was blaring again.

The instant I stepped into my bedroom, I was angry all over again. Ricki had dumped a pile of her clothes on my bed, and was lying on her own, reading one of the tabloid papers she and Aunt Norma had brought back from their last shopping trip.

I wasn't thinking clearly. I was too angry to control myself.

"I don't want your smelly clothes on my bed," I said, and I swept them off to the floor. In my mind, I went on with my tirade. Ricki, I thought, I hate the cologne you use—it smells like a public restroom. I hate the music you listen to, and, not to put too fine a point on it, I really hate you and your mother.

She sat up and dropped the paper. "Don't you push my clothes on the floor."

"Why not? That's where they were until you walked in here half an hour ago."

"Be careful," she said. "You be very careful."

"Or you'll what?" I asked. "You've been hinting around to my mother about Carey. I'm sick of putting up with your threats. Either you tell her or you don't, and I don't think you will. Don't forget, I was with you when I met Carey, and *your* mother didn't know where *you* were. I'll bet she doesn't want you hanging around with anyone like Dennis. What did you call him? A bad boy? How much do you know about bad boys, back in good old L.A.?"

Ricki flopped back down, laughing. "You sound like a dried-up old maid. You sound like a virgin."

I stared at her while my face burned. "You're disgusting," I said. "You make me want to throw up."

"Turn up the radio before you sneak out to see Carey," she said. "I like this music a lot."

I walked out. I couldn't sleep one more night in the same room with her, and there wasn't another available bed. For a moment I hesitated at the head of the stairs, considering my options, and then I hurried to Mom's room.

"Mom?"

"Come in," she said, and her bedside lamp went on as I opened the door. When she saw me, she exclaimed, "What's wrong?"

"I can't spend another night in the same room with Ricki," I said. "I hate her music, and she . . . she smells awful. And she snores."

Mom blinked. "You can change with Norma, then," she said. "I thought you girls might like to get to know each other better . . ."

"I can't remember ever hating anybody as much as I hate her," I blurted. "But Aunt Norma isn't here. If I change beds and she doesn't know about it until she comes in, she'll start in again, and I can't stand her, either. I wish we hadn't come here!"

Mom sat on the edge of her bed. "Everything's falling apart," she said wearily. She thought for a moment. "Okay, let's make a bed for you on the couch downstairs."

"No, because Aunt Norma will come in and see me and start yapping. I can't stand any more of this, Mom."

"Okay, here's another idea. How about making up a bed on the floor in one of the unused bedrooms? We've got plenty of blankets."

She was getting to her feet while she spoke, but I said, "Don't get up. How about the small bedroom at the head of the stairs?"

"You could take the mattress off your bed," Mom said. "Unless you don't want to go back into your bedroom."

"I'll get it," I said grimly.

"Are you sure you can manage?"

"Oh, yes," I said.

I stormed back down the hall and around the corner, and threw open my bedroom door. "I'm moving to another room," I said as I rolled up my bedding.

"Mmm," Ricki said. She was reading her paper again, and I swear she moved her lips as she studied the page.

I carried the bedding to my new room, then went back for my mattress. It was heavier than I had thought it would be.

"If you think I won't know when you sneak out tonight, think again," Ricki said as I struggled with the mattress.

I straightened up. "*You* don't think at all," I said. "And you don't scare me, either. Just remember—anything you do to me, I can do back to you."

With that, I gave one final tug, and my mattress popped out into the hall. I slammed the door and grinned.

But, yes, I was afraid of her.

Soon afterward, Aunt Norma came home. She climbed the stairs noisily and thumped down the hall to her room. "In bed already?" I heard her say to my mother. "I can't stand that car, Abby. Why do I have such terrible luck? It's just one thing after another with rentals." The door shut and I couldn't make out anything else.

I lay on the mattress, still dressed, my heart beating hard. After a long time, the bathroom door opened and closed, then opened again. Aunt Norma's voice whined along the hall. The bass notes of Ricki's music thudded in the walls.

I left, hurrying down the stairs and out the door. I'd be late this time. Would Carey wait for me? I was halfway down the hill, following the path that was striped with moonlight, when he stepped out in front of me.

"I was afraid you wouldn't come," he said softly.

I touched Mom's earring. "How could I not come?" I said.

He held out his hand. "I've got something for you."

He dropped the lost earring on my palm. "You found it!" I said.

"They had it in the lost and found," he said. "I went there this afternoon."

I put the earring on with shaking fingers. Maybe my luck would change now. Maybe, somehow, everything would turn out all right.

"Do you want to go to the amusement park?" Carey asked.

I looked across the beach at the lights. Pete and Dennis would be there. Pete, who'd hurt Owen. And I'd be in the way of Ellie and Meg. Ellie had openly resented me, and Meg's struggle to be nice to me was embarrassingly obvious.

"No. Is there somewhere else we could go?" I asked.

"We could climb up to the boardwalk and go to one of the cafes."

I didn't want to be stared at by strangers.

"Is there a place where we could just sit and talk?" I asked.

He laughed a little. "There are plenty of places in Royal Bay to sit and talk. Come on. I'll show you my favorite."

He took my hand and led me almost all the way to the end of the path, and then out into a small, rocky clearing that overlooked the water. It wasn't windy there. We sat on a smooth rock and leaned against a log. Ahead of us, the dark Sound stretched out to a distant, glimmering shore. A ship crossed in front of us, streaming light, its engines throbbing.

"I'd like to be on that ship," I said.

"Because it's going to Seattle?"

"Because it's going away from here," I said.

"You won't be staying much longer."

I sighed. "Part of me wishes I hadn't come. But then I wouldn't have met you."

He was silent for a moment, and then he said, "Maybe we would have met each other anyway."

"I don't see how."

Silence again. Finally he said, "You don't think it was strange? How I saw you and was sure I'd seen you before? How . . ."

"How what?" I asked. My voice shook.

He took my hand and held it against his chest. I could feel his heart beating.

"Do you believe in fate?" he asked.

Until that moment, I hadn't. "I do now," I said truthfully. "But this isn't a very kind fate—meeting each other and then saying good-bye."

"I've wondered what it will be like, when I'm in some other place and you're in Seattle. Will we ever think of each other at exactly the same moment? If I look up at the stars at night, will you be looking up, too?" He moved my hand up to his face and held it there. When he turned to look straight at me, my eyes filled with tears.

"Jane," he said simply

"I'll be looking up, too," I whispered.

"Promise me," he said.

"I promise you," I told him.

We sat there for a long time without speaking again. We could have used the time to talk—we still knew so little about each other. But it didn't seem necessary somehow. This wouldn't be the last time I'd see him, I was certain of that. There would be tomorrow night, and perhaps even another night after that. There, in that place and at that moment, I truly believed that something good might happen. I heard the water and the faint music from the carousel, and I didn't think of the house at the top of the hill or the problems seething within those walls.

After a while, Carey asked me why Ricki hadn't come with me. The question startled me, because I'd almost forgotten about her. "We aren't getting along very well," I said. "I didn't want her to come."

"Are you in trouble because of me?" he asked.

"My mother would like you," I said. "Except . . ."

"Except that I picked you up in an amusement park," he said. He rubbed his cheek against my hair. "It sounds terrible."

"I know. She would have a right to be upset. But I know she'd like you."

"If she had a chance," he said. "Does she like Owen?"

I sat up straight. "Yes. He's funny. She likes people who make her laugh."

"I could come by the house in a clown costume," he said, and laughed.

"It would take more than that," I said.

"Where did you meet Owen?"

"In his uncle's restaurant," I said. I took a deep breath and said, "Pete beat him up. Did you know that?"

Carey slung his arm over my shoulder and hugged me. "I heard about it, and I was sorry. That Pete—he's got a rotten temper and he takes it out on other people. He was angry with the basketball players from Seattle because of something that happened at the playoffs. And Owen was hanging around with them. I've never known Pete to give up a grudge, because that might mean he'd be giving up a chance for a fight. I was glad when I heard that he hadn't hurt Owen worse than he did."

"But Pete's your friend," I said.

"His mother is my mother's best friend, and that's about it," Carey said. "I'm sort of an outsider, maybe because I spend part of the time with my dad. I wish Pete had left Owen alone. If I'd been there, I'd have stopped him. He'll listen to me. Sometimes, anyway. But I wish your cousin would stay away from him and Dennis."

"Maybe *they* should stay away from *her*," I said. "I think she's more trouble."

"We'll let the world take care of itself," he said. "Come on. I'll walk you home."

And kiss me at the door, I thought. Oh, please, kiss me at the door.

He did. He didn't say anything, but just kissed me once, and then once more.

I went inside. The lights were on again! I hadn't noticed and now it was too late. Mom waited for me on the couch.

"You should have invited him in," she said.

Chapter Thirteen

It seemed to me that the world had stopped. I couldn't breathe or think.

Nothing would work except the truth. "I wanted you to meet Carey," I said, my voice trembling. "But I didn't think you'd like him because I met him at the amusement park."

"You're right about that," Mom said. "You know how I feel about the place. And you know how your father and I feel about your spending time with boys we don't know. That's been a rule since you started dating. Jane, I'm having trouble even believing that you'd sneak out of the house. That's Ricki's style, not yours."

Here was a chance to blame the whole thing on Ricki, but I wouldn't do it. I hadn't been forced to go with her. She hadn't tied me up and dragged me there.

"I knew you'd be angry," I said. "I'm sorry."

Mom sighed. "Sorry won't cut it. What you've done is so dangerous, so stupid, that being sorry isn't a solution. It's as if you lost all common sense."

Obviously I had. What was I supposed to say?

"Carey's a nice boy," I began.

"So nice that he picks up strange girls in a nasty, rundown amusement park in an old cannery town," Mom said. "And by the way, I can see that you've got a mate for my old earring."

"Carey found it in his mother's antique shop," I said. I fingered the earring nervously. "Last night Ricki pulled it off when we were on the Ferris wheel. She threw it out on the ground, but Carey got it back today from the lost and found." I was babbling and I knew it. But now that I'd been caught, I wanted to tell everything.

"History is repeating itself," Mom said. She rubbed her forehead gingerly. "Well, why shouldn't Norma have told her daughter what she did to me? After all, I told you, didn't I?"

"She should have been ashamed to tell anybody," I said angrily. Mom only looked at me.

I groaned. "Okay. I know you hate this. But I don't know how to fix it. I can find Carey tomorrow and bring him back to the house so you can see what he's like. He wanted to meet you. His feelings were hurt when he found out that I'd been sneaking out to see him. He'd thought you knew about him and . . ."

"And didn't care that my fifteen-year-old daughter picked up boys," she finished. "Well, that's wonderful, isn't it?"

I bit my lip so hard that it hurt. "What do you want me to do?" I asked.

"For one thing, I don't want you going back to that horrible place," she said. "But that must be obvious to you already."

"Can I bring him to meet you?"

"I can live without that experience, thank you," she said. She got to her feet slowly, as if her legs and back hurt.

"Can I see him tomorrow night, then?"

"Would it do any good if I said no?" she asked. She turned to face me, and her eyes burned holes in me.

I'm terribly sorry, but it won't do any good, I thought. I opened my mouth and closed it again. What could I say that wouldn't make her angrier than she already was?

"I see," Mom said. She turned her back on me and walked toward the stairs. She didn't look back or say goodnight.

I'd been dumped by my own mother! I was so angry—so humiliated—that all I could do was cry.

Ricki! She had done this! It was *her* fault!

I hurried up the stairs. Ahead of me, Mom disappeared into her room. I couldn't hear Ricki's radio playing, but I knew better than to believe that she was sleeping.

I threw open our bedroom door. The room was dark. I flipped the light switch on and off several times.

"Ricki?" I yelled. "Ricki! I know you aren't sleeping! You've been eavesdropping the whole time, haven't you?"

The lump under her covers heaved, and Ricki sat up, hair mussed and makeup clotted.

"I warned you," she singsonged. "You shouldn't have made me mad."

"Why did you do it?" I demanded. "Why did you tell her? What was the point? I didn't do anything to hurt you."

"You took Carey!" she said. "I decided that I wanted him, but *you* took him."

"Boys aren't for *taking!*" I said. "He isn't a thing, a toy, a trophy. He makes up his own mind."

She didn't hear me. Her face was stiff with hatred. "I'm used to getting what I want," she said. "I told you that I don't like girls, so it doesn't bother me a bit when I do what I have to do. You *made* me do it! This is *your* fault!"

I shook my head, amazed. "But you didn't get anything out of it. Not anything! Can't you see that? Carey still doesn't like you, and he never will. You betrayed me for nothing."

"Oh, it wasn't for nothing, Janie girl," Ricki said. "I loved every minute of it. You should have seen your mother's face when I told her where you were and what you were doing."

"And what about *your* mother's face?" I asked.

"Norma loved every minute of it, too. She told your mom that you had inherited all her bad habits. Norma said that this was a good payback for what had happened to Mark."

I stared, dumbfounded. "Who is Mark?"

Ricki laughed. "What? Your mommy didn't tell you about Mark? About how she stole him from Norma, and how everybody knew what a bitch your mother was, to take the boy her sister was going to marry?"

"She would never do something like that," I said. "She would never betray another woman, especially her own sister. She sticks up for other women, she doesn't turn on them. But I can't expect someone like you to understand something that decent."

It was Ricki's turn to stare. "You're kidding, right? You think your mother's a saint, don't you?"

"I know that she does the right thing, always."

"If you believe that, then you'd better ask her about Mark," Ricki said. "I'd love to be around to hear the answer."

I left the room and slammed the door behind me, hard enough to hurt my arm.

It seemed to me that I lay awake all night, but sometime around dawn I fell asleep and didn't wake up until late. I dressed quickly and hurried downstairs. I wasn't eager to run into trouble, but I wanted to have whatever trouble was coming to be over and done with as soon as possible, so I didn't have to keep holding my breath and looking behind me.

Mom was packing pots and pans in the kitchen. She looked up as I came in.

"Norma got up before I did and she took my car," she said in a flat, sick voice.

I blinked, unbelieving. "She took *your* car? She stole your keys and took your car? Is Ricki with her?"

"I looked in Ricki's room. She's still there, sleeping."

"Where did Aunt Norma go?" I asked.

"Who knows? Shopping, probably. Nothing ever seems to interfere with shopping or lunching out or . . ." Mom's eyes filled with tears.

"Your headache is worse, isn't it?" I asked.

She didn't answer my question. Instead, she said, "I'll walk into town pretty soon and call Mrs. Soriano. Maybe the movers can come for the furniture earlier than she thought. Maybe we can get out of here before I go completely crazy."

She didn't say anything about Carey and I didn't ask. I knew better.

Silently, I got the cat food and went out to feed the poor thing. The saucer was empty again, and in a far corner of the yard, under an old lilac bush, the cat crouched and watched.

"Kitty?" I called.

He didn't run away, but he didn't come closer either.

I ate breakfast only because Mom insisted, but I wasn't hungry. When I was done, we walked to the nearest phone so she could call Mrs. Soriano, but she didn't get the news she'd hoped for. When she hung up, she looked even more tired than she had before.

"Norma has already been there," Mom said. "She told Mrs. Soriano that she was calling her lawyer and having the sale stopped. Mrs. Soriano said she didn't want trouble, so she's cancelled the truck. They won't even be coming tomorrow."

"Can Aunt Norma stop the sale?" I asked.

"She can't stop the things from being sold," Mom said. "The court ordered it done. But Norma has scared off Mrs. Soriano, at least for the time being."

"What are you going to do now?" I asked.

Mom closed her eyes for a long moment. "First, I'm going to get a cup of coffee," she said. "Then I'm going back to the house to wait for Norma and see if I can talk some sense into her."

The morning was cool, but we sat at a table outside the coffee shop. Mom ordered black coffee and I asked for hot chocolate.

While we waited, I said, "I suppose you heard Ricki and me arguing last night."

"Everyone in town did," Mom said. She smiled a little, but she didn't look at me.

"Then you heard her say something about someone called Mark," I said. I avoided looking at her, too.

"Yes."

"I didn't believe what she said. Was Mark the one who gave you the earrings?"

The waitress brought our hot drinks, and Mom waited until she was gone.

"Mark wasn't the one who gave me the earrings," she said. "Mark was a boy Norma had dated in college. I barely knew him and never gave him a thought. Norma and I lived in different dorms and had little or nothing to do with each other. Then Mark got in touch with me and said he wasn't going to see Norma again. He said terrible things about her. He called me back several times and finally asked me to go out with him."

"Did you go?" I asked.

"Not at first. I didn't like him much, but he was so persistent that I finally gave in and agreed to have an early dinner with him. It was a terrible mistake. He got serious, from just that one date. He was frightening, actually. I refused to see him again, but he followed me everywhere. When I'd leave a class, he'd be there. He hung around the dorm until other girls complained. He left messages for me, sent letters, and phoned constantly."

"That's scary, Mom," I said. "That's stalking."

"I ended up moving out of my dorm and staying with friends in their apartment. When he found me there, I was so frightened that I dropped out of school—that was spring quarter—and came back to Royal Bay. I made the mistake of telling my mother, and she wrote all the details to Norma. Norma confronted Mark and told him where I was. Both of them came here when spring quarter was over. Mark showed up at the house, but I refused to see him. In fact, as soon as he left, I asked Mrs. Phare to drive me to Port Shasta, and I caught the Anacortes ferry and then took a bus back to Seattle. I was so fed up with my mother and Norma that I didn't return to Royal Bay for years, not until after your father and I were married."

"What about Mark?" I asked.

"Norma sent me a newspaper clipping. Mark had fallen from one of the amusement park rides and died from his injuries. Norma had written 'murderer' in red ink across the clipping. She sent copies to several of my friends."

"But that's ridiculous!" I exclaimed. "You didn't have anything to do with what happened to him."

"No, but Norma is fond of melodrama. For years, on the anniversary of Mark's death, she'd send me a hysterical letter blaming me. Mark fell—it was an accident, not suicide. And not murder."

"But she doesn't send those letters now, does she?" I asked.

Mom laughed a little. "No, Norma doesn't have that long of an attention span. And her marriages and divorces have kept her busy, I suppose."

"But she told Ricki," I said.

Mom shrugged. "Oh, sure. She probably enjoyed reliving everything."

"I can see why you hate the park," I said reluctantly.

"I'd hate it anyway," she said. "It's a nasty place."

I took a deep breath. I couldn't disagree with her. "Let me bring Carey to the house today," I said. "I can probably find him. He works in his mother's shop. I'd like you to know him, to see that he isn't awful."

Mom's face flushed. "I can't do that. I can't pretend that I'm not angry about what you've been doing. We'll be gone in another couple of days, and you'll have to say good-bye to him anyway."

How could I stay away from Carey? We had one more chance to spend time together, maybe two, and then we wouldn't see each other again.

"Mom . . ." I began.

She held up one hand in protest. "Don't," she said. "Don't lie to me anymore. I can't take it."

"I wasn't going to lie," I said. "I was going to tell you the truth. I want to see him again. I just wish you'd say it was all right."

She shook her head. "I can't say something is all right when it's all wrong, and you know that. I'm asking you to grow up, Jane."

I looked down at my clasped hands and would not speak.

This was a hopeless situation.

We worked hard the rest of the day, stacking boxes filled with household goods in the living room. We vacuumed every room, cleaned the bathrooms and kitchen one last time, and spent the last of the afternoon working in the flower beds. We only spoke to each other when we had to. We'd never had a quarrel that lasted so long before, and I didn't know how to bring it to an end.

She was angry with me because I'd sneaked out of the house. And I was angry because she had never told me how bad things were between her and Aunt Norma. If I had known, I wouldn't have gone near Royal Bay.

But then, I wouldn't have met Carey.

This wasn't something I could sort out.

While we worked in the yard, the white cat watched us closely from the shrubbery, and when I brought out more food, he ate greedily while I stood almost within reach. I thought I heard him purring. His coat was filthy and matted; clearly he was a stray. I mentioned this to Mom, and then regretted it, because when she turned to look at him, her eyes brimmed with tears.

"I think you're right," she said. "Why are people so cruel?"

Her face was haggard. I had never seen her like this. What had happened to my strong, calm mother? I barely recognized this exhausted woman who cried—and lost her temper—so easily. I wasn't even certain I liked her. How could I rely on someone like her?

But then, wasn't she wondering how she could rely on me?

Throughout the day, Ricki came and went on mysterious errands without speaking to us, and we didn't speak to her. After the last time she left, around four o'clock, she didn't return.

Mom and I found nothing to talk about. Tension hung over the house like poisonous smoke.

We walked into town for an early dinner, and Owen greeted us enthusiastically.

"I've been given parole," he said as he put our water glasses down, hardly spilling a drop.

"You're going back to Seattle," I said.

"Tomorrow morning," he said. "I got lucky. Not only has my mother fired me, but my uncle has, too. He says I'm the worst help he's ever had, and he'd rather deal with a fire or an earthquake because then there's the chance of a happy ending. So give me your address and phone number in Seattle, and I'll be ready and waiting for you when you get back."

"Your bruises look better," I said.

"Don't change the subject," he said. "Give me your phone number at least, and I'll have it tattooed on the back of my hand for easy reference."

Mom wrote our phone number on a napkin and handed it to him. "We'd love to see you and your mother again," she said.

It won't help, I thought. It won't make me forget Carey.

We had a good meal and walked home in silence. I couldn't think of anything to say. I wondered what she was thinking, and what she expected me to do that evening. Did she think I'd bother to sneak out again? Or would she wait for me to say I was leaving for the amusement park?

We were nearly home when Mom said, "There's my car, in the driveway."

Aunt Norma was back. Mom walked a little faster, and when I saw the grim look on her face, I smiled to myself. Maybe my aunt would finally get at least a small part of what she deserved. Maybe Mom was going to stand up for herself at last.

As soon as we walked in, Aunt Norma hurried into the living room from the kitchen. "Here you are," she said. "We've been waiting and waiting, wondering what you expected us to do for dinner. There isn't a thing to eat in this house except breakfast cereal and stale bread. What are we supposed to do?"

"I expected you not to steal my car, for one thing," Mom said.

Ricki, standing behind her mother, said, "Norma didn't steal your car. She left you a note in the kitchen, telling you she had to use it."

"I saw no note," Mom said.

"Well, it was there," Aunt Norma said. Her cheeks were red. She was lying.

"Give me my car keys," Mom said, and she held out her hand.

"I don't know where they are," Aunt Norma said, and she sniffed and dabbed at her nose with a wadded-up tissue. "If

I've lost them, it's because you upset me so much. This is your fault."

"I talked to Mrs. Soriano today," Mom said as she let her hand fall to her side. "She told me what you said to her."

"I didn't do anything except try to take care of myself and my little girl," Aunt Norma whined. "I leave boring business details to other people. But I need a lawyer to stick up for me now, since I can't trust you. God knows why, but you've resented me all your life. My friends told me you'd try to cheat me out of my inheritance."

"Stop it," Mom said. "Stop acting like a helpless two-year-old. Whether you like it or not, everything here is going to be sold, except for the keepsakes you were told you could take. Make up your mind what you want, and then stop interfering."

"I'd take the china that Mother promised to me, if I could find all the pieces," Aunt Norma said. "I'd like to know what happened to the missing bowls, and that big platter."

Mom pushed back her hair. "I don't know where they are. I suppose they broke and Mother threw them out. You know she didn't hang on to things when they weren't usable anymore."

"So *you* say," Aunt Norma muttered. "You had access to this house for more than two years. How do I know what you did?"

"I came here once, after the funeral," Mom said, falling neatly into Aunt Norma's trap and defending herself again. "I arranged with the Phares to check on the house and make sure everything was all right."

"Then maybe the Phares took the china," Aunt Norma said. "I never did like them, and neither did Mother. They could have stolen anything here . . ."

"They didn't *want* anything here!" Mom exclaimed. "Good grief, Norma. Open your eyes and look around you. Mother didn't own anything of great value."

"So you say," Aunt Norma said. "But when could I ever believe you about anything? My friends warned me about trusting you."

Mom walked away without speaking. I followed her into the kitchen and found her leaning over the sink, splashing cold water on her face. She looked so ill that I was frightened. Sometimes her headaches were so bad that she threw up.

"Take one of your headache pills," I whispered.

"I've run out," she said. She pressed the heels of her hands against her eyes. "My god, this is insanity. I fall into every trap she sets. I can't seem to learn anything about dealing with her."

Aunt Norma appeared in the doorway and said, "Ricki and I haven't had anything to eat. What are we supposed to do for dinner?"

"Take your own car and drive into town to eat," I shouted. "Go on! Get out of here!"

"Don't you tell me what to do, you nasty little brat!" Aunt Norma shouted right back at me. "Don't think my Ricki hasn't told me some things about you, things that might interest your mother very much. Who do you think you are, anyway?"

"Get out of this house," I said softly. "Get out right now. You're making my mother sick."

"Come on, Norma," Ricki said. "Let's drive into Port Shasta and get a real meal."

"Not in Mom's car," I said.

"I can't stand that rental car because . . ." Aunt Norma began.

"Give me our keys," I yelled. I took two steps toward her and stuck out my hand.

Aunt Norma backed up two steps, reached into her pocket, and threw the keys at me, hard. I caught them, although my palm stung.

"You're just like your mother," she said. "You're exactly like her."

"I hope so," I retaliated. "I'd rather be like her than like you."

We stood there, the four of us, while several seconds ticked by. Then Aunt Norma turned and left. Ricki shot me a smirk and followed. I waited until the front door slammed, and then I turned to my mother.

"What are we going to do?" I asked.

She shook her head. "I don't know. I can't think straight anymore. She drives me crazy."

"Then let's get out of here before they come back," I said. "We can stay in one of the motels. We can drive there right now, and we'll call Dad and ask him what he thinks we should do."

"I can't bother your father again with this," she said. "He's gone through enough these last two years. Norma's my sister."

"She's *nobody's* sister," I stormed. "She's nobody's anything.

Come on. We're grabbing our pajamas and getting out of here, at least for tonight."

I suppose, dimly, I thought I'd still see Carey that night, that we'd find each other the way we always did.

I suppose I thought that there was still a chance everything could turn out all right.

Chapter Fourteen

I left Mom downstairs, lying on the couch. On my way to her bedroom, I decided that I'd pack all of our things. There was no reason for us to continue spending our nights in the house—and putting up with our relatives.

I stuffed Mom's things into her suitcase without bothering to fold anything. After I closed it, I remembered her personal items, so I rushed into the bathroom, grabbed up the few things that belonged to Mom and me, rushed back and shoved them into the outside pocket on the suitcase.

It didn't take long to pack my clothes and *Ishmael.* I ran back downstairs with our bags, got our coats out of the closet, and said, "We're all set."

"It looks as if you took more than our pajamas," Mom said.

"I packed everything," I said, and I explained why.

Mom nodded wearily. "You're right. Okay, then, let's go."

"Are you well enough to drive?" I asked, worried.

Mom laughed a little, and winced. "I couldn't make it all the way back to Seattle, but I'll be okay for a short trip. Let's try that place across the street from the restaurant we like. But first, I'd better leave Norma a note."

"No notes," I said. "It will do her good to wonder." I pulled on Mom's arm before she overruled me.

When we got in the car, Mom said, "What's that awful smell?"

"Ricki," I said. "That's her perfume."

We checked into the hotel, and as soon as we reached our room, Mom ordered tea from room service. But she fell asleep almost instantly, and when the tea came, I drank it by myself, looking out the window and watching people come and go.

Carey would be waiting for me at the amusement park. Or perhaps he'd be halfway up the hill. He would wonder where I was, and if I had changed my mind about him.

Mom was sleeping soundly, so I could sneak out to meet him. But what if she woke and found me gone? I wasn't sure she was strong enough to get angry about anything, but I knew I couldn't bear to see any more of her tears.

And if I left to meet Carey, it would be the worst sort of betrayal. For the first time, my mother's code of behavior seemed an intolerable burden to me. Ricki would have left her sick mother without hesitation. I couldn't do it. But I was tempted.

"I hate this town," I said softly, to myself. Part of me had changed since I arrived, and I wasn't sure the change was good.

I woke the next morning to find Mom dressed in different clothes, lying on the bed with a wet washcloth over her eyes.

"You've still got the headache," I said. "Would you like breakfast from room service? Or just tea?"

"Just tea. But you get everything you want."

She drifted off again into a sick sleep, and I stood at the window, watching.

We were on the second floor. In front of the restaurant across the street, I saw a black bird with a brown head perched on a tree branch. Beneath her, barely visible, there was a much smaller bird in a nest.

"Darned cowbird," I said, and I rapped my knuckles on the window. If the larger bird heard me, she ignored me.

"What?" Mom mumbled sleepily.

"Sorry I woke you, Mom," I said. "But there's a cowbird across the street, just waiting for a chance to lay her egg in another bird's nest."

Mom got up on one elbow. "I remember what you told me about them."

I rapped on the window again. The brown-headed bird ignored me. "It makes me sick to think about the cowbird's chick pushing the other babies out of the nest."

Mom lay back down gingerly. "Nature is cruel," she said.

Life is cruel, I thought. And selfish.

I ordered a big breakfast for myself, and tea for Mom. She drank a little but didn't get up.

"You aren't well enough to go back to the house," I said. "Maybe we should call a doctor."

"I'll be better after a while," she said. "I've got to go back and finish up. And somehow, I'll have to find a way to talk Norma into letting Mrs. Soriano take all the stuff. Maybe our being gone overnight will scare some sense into her."

I laughed. "No, she'll be angry about that, too."

When I finished breakfast, I went back to the window. The cowbird was gone. I couldn't see the bird in the nest, either.

That old stray cat might have been catching birds, but he couldn't have been very good at it. He was terribly thin.

The cat!

"Mom, I've got to go back to the house right now," I said urgently. "The cat will be waiting for its breakfast."

Mom propped herself up again. "It's not going to help much. When we're gone, the cat will be right back where he was before."

"No," I said. "No! We'll take him back to Seattle with us. Henry might like a friend."

"We could take him home," Mom said slowly. "That would be the one good thing about this trip. Do you think you'll be able to catch him?"

I wasn't sure, but I told Mom that I knew I could.

"I'll go now," I said.

I let myself in the front door of Grandmother's house with Mom's key. The place was silent. I thought Aunt Norma and Ricki were still asleep, and I drew a deep breath.

The living room curtains were closed, but I saw the litter of crumbs on the coffee table and a pop can on the floor. A cracker had been ground into the carpet.

Well, *I* wasn't going to clean the room again.

I hurried through the dining room to the kitchen, passing boxes that had been emptied out on the floor. The mess made me sick, when I remembered how much work Mom and I had done.

In the kitchen, Aunt Norma looked up from her place at the table. "Where have you been?" she demanded. "Where is Abby? I still can't find the missing pieces of china. And . . ."

I ignored her and opened the refrigerator to get the cat food. She followed me outside.

"Where have you been?" she demanded again.

I bent to pick up the saucer, but she grabbed it. "Look at that. It's part of the Royal Doulton set! The gold rim is chipped now . . ."

"It always was," I said. I took it from her and walked toward the shrubbery. "Kitty? Kitty?" I could barely see him. His round golden eyes stared out at me without blinking while I dumped the last of the cat food on the saucer.

"I don't want that cat around here!" Aunt Norma yelled. "I'm allergic to them."

Her screeching was frightening the cat. I was afraid I would never be able to catch him as long as she was out in the yard.

"Be quiet and go back in the house," I said.

"I want to know where you and your mother have been," Aunt Norma said. She started toward me, her silk robe dragging on the grass. "How dare she run out on me and leave me here with nothing to eat and all this work to be done?"

"Most of the work is finished," I said. "No thanks to you or your lazy daughter. Eat at a restaurant if you're hungry."

"I want to know where Abby is," Aunt Norma said. "She's got a lot to answer for."

I wasn't going to tell her anything.

"Are you deaf?" Aunt Norma cried.

I lost my temper completely. "You cowbird!" I said. "You're a parasite. Everything is all about *you,* isn't it? You don't care about anybody except yourself."

Aunt Norma stopped moving toward me. "What did you call me?" Her face was purple with rage.

"Go back in the house," I said. "I want to catch the cat, and I'll never get it as long as you're out here, bellowing so the whole town can hear you. But I suppose they're used to you by now."

I turned my back. The door slammed.

I was alone in the backyard with the cat. My hands were shaking. I shouldn't have talked to my aunt that way. She was old and pathetic, and probably as scared about her future as any woman raising a daughter alone. But she was so selfish!

"Look what I've got, kitty," I said as I knelt by the shrubbery. I put the saucer down and backed up a couple of steps, then knelt to wait.

After a long moment, the cat moved forward cautiously and peered out at me. I stayed silent and waited.

He waited.

What was I going to do? Mom was too sick to deal with my crazy aunt—and I hated my crazy cousin. I had to get us back to Seattle. Should I call Dad? It would take a couple of hours for him to drive to the ferry, then there would be the long ferry ride across the Sound, then the drive to Royal Bay. Even if he left right away, he couldn't get here before late afternoon.

Mom and I could escape and reach home by that time.

Home, free of Aunt Norma and Ricki.

But what about Carey? I hadn't seen him the night before, and he must have wondered what had happened. I didn't want to give up the chance to see him once or twice again.

The back door opened. "Jane!" Aunt Norma bawled. "Tell Abby to get back here."

I knew what to do.

I nodded at Aunt Norma, and she took it as consent, which was what I had planned. She went inside again.

The morning was cool, but I stripped off my denim jacket and laid it across my knees. Then I nudged the cat food a little closer to the shrubbery. The cat watched. I called him softly and waited.

He crept out slowly, cautiously and began to eat. I waited until he had finished more than half the food, and then I simply picked up my jacket and dropped it over him. Quickly, before he could escape, I gathered him up in my arms.

"We're going home," I whispered to him. "Henry's waiting to meet you."

On the way to the hotel, I hoped I'd see Carey somewhere so I could explain. But the only familiar person I saw was Owen, passing me in a car. He waved, the car turned the corner, and he was gone, on his way back to Seattle.

The cat lay quietly in my arms, purring, as if he knew what I had decided must be done, and he was glad.

I hoped Carey would be in his mother's shop, but if he wasn't, I would leave my name and address with her. Maybe he'd write to me. Maybe he wouldn't bother. I couldn't let myself think about it until I was safely home, because I was afraid I'd start crying and never stop.

I pushed open the door and a bell tinkled in the back of the shop. A tall, slender woman came out and looked inquiringly at me and the cat. I asked for Carey.

He must have heard, because he came through the door behind her.

"Jane," he said. "I didn't know if . . ."

"We have to leave today," I said quickly. "Mom's sick, and I found this stray cat, and most of the work is done . . ."

I was babbling. If I had prepared something to say, I couldn't remember it any longer.

The woman left the room, smiling a little.

"You're going back to Seattle now?" Carey asked.

I nodded. "I'm sorry I didn't meet you last night, but we moved into a hotel, and Mom was awfully sick."

"And you've got a cat?"

I explained about the stray. I don't know if he was listening, because his gaze never left my face.

"Wait here," he said. "I've got something for you."

He went into the back room and returned almost immediately. "Hold out your hand," he said.

I held out my right hand and he opened his over it, spilling a dozen moonstones into my palm.

Some were white, some silver. I saw a large pink one and two small peach-colored ones. One was blue and no larger than a pea.

"They are beautiful," I whispered. "Where did you get them?"

"I found them in our storage room," he said. "My mother gave them to me so I could give them to you. You could have them made into a necklace, she said. Or a bracelet."

I closed my fingers over the beautiful stones. "Thank you," I whispered.

"They're to remember me by," he said.

"Write to me," I said. "I'll answer you." I gave him my address, and he wrote it on a scrap of paper which he put in his wallet. Then he took my free hand and touched my fingertips, one by one. "Think of me," he said. He kissed me once, quickly, while the cat watched, big-eyed.

I hurried away, looked back to see him watching me soberly, and then I turned the corner.

I let the cat loose in our room and watched while he explored nervously, his claws catching in the carpet.

"I'm not sure the hotel will let us keep him here," Mom said.

"It's not going to be a problem," I said. Now was the time to tell her. "We're leaving today. Right now, if you're well enough. Think of this, Mom. We can be home before dinner. We'll be gone from here and never have to come back."

"But I have to finish . . ."

"No, no," I said. "*Aunt Norma has to finish.* You said yourself you don't care if she gets everything. So leave it to her."

"But the court ordered everything to be sold and the money divided," Mom said.

"If you go now, nobody will put you in jail, right?" I asked.

"Of course not," Mom said. "But there could be complications."

"Let Aunt Norma straighten them out. Let her get in touch with Mrs. Soriano or somebody else—her wonderful, helpful friends back in Los Angeles."

Mom shook her head. "Jane, I can't do this. I can't just walk out and leave things . . ."

"This time you can," I said. "Mom, please. You're sick—worse than you've ever been. And you've changed. Look what's happened to you since we got here."

"Look what's happened to *you* since we got here!" Mom cried.

We stared furiously at each other. We'd never quarreled like this before. I could scarcely believe that she would respond to my concern for her with an attack.

We had frightened the cat. He crouched under a chair, his eyes wild.

Mom saw him, too, and her eyes filled with tears again. "Where does it end?" she asked. "It's this town, this horrible, depressing place. I worked so hard to escape from it, and here I am again. Only

THESMAN, JEAN *The Moonstones.* Viking, 1998 [208p]
ISBN 0-670-87959-2 $15.99   SEP   1998
Reviewed from galleys   R Gr. 6-9

Jane accompanies her mother, Abby, to Puget Sound to help prepare her deceased
grandmother's house for sale; Mom's sister, Norma, and her daughter, Ricki, are
supposed to help as well, but instead they preen, complain, and tear open family
wounds, compromising Jane's closeness with Abby. Wild and flirtatious Ricki
entices Jane to sneak out at night to the seedy, forbidden amusement park, where
Ricki deftly maneuvers among a clique of local teens and Jane falls for intelligent,
handsome Carey, who always skirts along the edge of the pack. Ricki, unfazed that
Norma might learn of their escapades, blackmails Jane with the threat of disclos-
ing their nocturnal jaunts and torments her with family secrets concerning the
animosity between their mothers. Norma and Ricki epitomize the self-absorbed,
vicious villainesses readers love to hate; their dysfunction stands in bold relief against
Jane and Abby's temporarily strained but ultimately loving relationship. Although
the aura of mystery and danger with which Thesman surrounds Carey proves to be
deceptive (he's really quite a nice, ordinary guy who hangs with some weird ac-
quaintances), his blossoming romance with Jane should satisfy junior-high girls
looking for some cathartic amour. EB